"Shut the door!"

Giving her a none-too-gentle shove, Chet removed her from his path and stormed into the room.

Molly watched, open-mouthed, as he circled the rocker and gripped the high back with both hands. She had the distinct impression he wanted to throw it.

"Chet, what in the world?"

The deadly fury in his eyes was enough to make her gasp in alarm. "Have you lost your mind? How dare you force your way in here!"

"I've had enough of your playacting," he shot back. So furious he could barely contain himself, he kept his fingers clamped to the chair back. "I don't know what your game is, Molly!" he shouted. "But I intend to find out before I leave here."

Molly felt the blood leave her face. He would have had to know eventually, but not like this. Oh, God, not like this....

Dear Reader,

When two people fall in love, the world is suddenly new and exciting, and it's that same excitement we bring to you in Silhouette Intimate Moments. These are stories with scope and grandeur. The characters lead lives we all dream of, and everything they do reflects the wonder of being in love.

Longer and more sensuous than most romances, Silhouette Intimate Moments novels take you away from everyday life and let you share the magic of love. Adventure, glamour, drama, even suspense— these are the passwords that let you into a world where love has a power beyond the ordinary, where the best authors in the field today create stories of love and commitment that will stay with you always.

In coming months, look for novels by your favorite authors: Linda Howard, Heather Graham Pozzessere, Emilie Richards and Kathleen Korbel, to name just a few. And whenever you buy books, look for all the Silhouette Intimate Moments, love stories for today's woman by today's woman.

Leslie J. Wainger
Senior Editor and Editorial Coordinator

JEANNE STEPHENS

Summer Heat

SILHOUETTE·INTIMATE·MOMENTS®

Published by Silhouette Books New York

America's Publisher of Contemporary Romance

SILHOUETTE BOOKS
300 East 42nd St., New York, N.Y. 10017

SUMMER HEAT

ISBN: 0-373-07380-1

First Silhouette Books printing April 1991

Printed in the U.S.A.

Books by Jeanne Stephens

Silhouette Romance

Mexican Nights #22
Wonder and Wild Desire #80
Sweet Jasmine #189
Broken Dreams #531

Silhouette Special Edition

Bride in Barbados #30
Pride's Possession #47
The Splendored Sky #84
No Other Love #108
Mandy's Song #217
Coming Home #252
This Long Winter Past #295
A Few Shining Hours #308
Return to Eden #372
Neptune Summer #431

Silhouette Desire

Sharing California #504

Silhouette Intimate Moments

Reckless Surrender #14
Memories #38
Whispers on the Wind #127
The Haunted Season #161
Mistress of Cliff House #200
Dangerous Choices #259
At Risk #308
Hiding Places #353
Summer Heat #380

JEANNE STEPHENS

loves to travel, but she's always glad to get home to Oklahoma. This incurable romantic and mother of three loves reading ("I'll read anything!" she says), needlework, photography, long walks—during which she works out her latest books—and, of course, her own romantic hero: her husband.

Chapter 1

Molly felt a prickle of foreboding. Had it been a mistake coming here?

Only a flash, and then it was gone. Like a dust devil disappearing over the horizon.

From her vantage point, Sunset didn't appear to be much of a threat. For that matter, it wasn't much of a town. The haphazard cluster of low buildings surrounded by prairie neither surprised nor disappointed her. She planned to stay only long enough to learn the truth, as painful as that might be.

She turned off the highway, taking the graveled lane to Jeb's Gas 'n' Snax on the edge of the little west Texas settlement. Pulling up to the self-serve island, she switched off the engine and watched another layer of dust settle on the hood of her compact car. The car had been white when she'd left Dallas early that morning. Now in midafternoon it was dirt brown, as though the land were reaching out to envelop it, as it claimed everything here.

Her skin and mouth felt as gritty as her automobile looked. Sighing, she tried to work some of the stiffness out of her neck and shoulders. Her flowered cotton dress, she noticed resignedly, looked as though it had spent the past month wadded into a ball and stuffed in an exceedingly small container.

As she climbed out, the July heat hit her with the force of a physical blow. Almost immediately, she felt perspiration popping out on her forehead and between her breasts.

After positioning the gas nozzle in the fuel tank opening, she gazed out over the monotonously treeless landscape. West Texas was harsh, flat country, sunbaked and dust-stung in summer, whipped by frigid winds in winter. It bred tough, resilient people.

Molly loved her native Texas and was proud of its colorful history. There were times when her enthusiasm for the subject caused her to wax eloquent with outsiders. On such an occasion, one of her Missouri cousins had remarked, "Texas isn't a state, it's a religion." Just another joke about the healthy ego of native Texans. Molly had never felt a need to apologize for that.

Feeling as she did, she had never believed that the words attributed to a legendary trail driver of the 1800s had ever actually been uttered. "If I owned hell and Texas," the cowboy had reputedly said, "I'd rent out Texas and live in hell." Now an inkling of doubt colored her former disbelief. She could very well imagine a drover saying the words after driving a herd of thirsty longhorns across west Texas in July.

Of course, she was predisposed to find fault with Sunset. This was where her father had died—"accidentally," according to those who passed official judgment on such matters. She had come to find out how it had *really* happened.

She paid for the gas, and asked the bald man behind the counter for directions to the Hammond Motel.

He handed over her change and hitched his sagging trousers up over a potbelly. "A block west of Main Street on Second. You can't miss it. The highway will take you right into town on Main."

Molly thanked him and went to the ladies' room to wash the grit off her face, run a comb through her short, naturally curly black hair and apply a dab of lip gloss. She studied her reflection in the mirror and decided she still looked frazzled and tired enough to drop. But a comb and makeup wouldn't change that. She needed a shower, a shampoo and a nap.

Back in her car, she started the engine to get the air conditioner going, but didn't immediately shift into drive. Small-town residents were curious about strangers, and she still hadn't come up with a plausible reason for being in Sunset. She didn't know what she would do if there was no vacancy at the Hammond Motel, and with the recent drilling activity going on in the Sunset oil field, it was possible there would be no available rooms. If there were other motels in Sunset, they could be full, too. She frowned, wondering how she would proceed if there wasn't a single room to let in town.

The oil field, covering hundreds of acres west of town, had brought her father to Sunset; George Backus had been a geologist. At the time of his death, he'd been "sitting" a well for Delaney Drilling Company.

Fortunately, no one could connect Molly Sinclair to her father by name, since she'd kept her ex-husband's when they'd divorced six years ago. It had seemed simpler at the time.

She'd been looking forward to spending a couple of weeks of her summer vacation with her father in Sunset when the word came in April that he was dead. He'd been driving while intoxicated, they'd said, and had lost control of his car, which had plunged into Sunset Lake.

At the time, she'd been too stunned to ask any questions. It had been all she could manage to arrange for the body to be shipped to Dallas for the funeral service and burial. To get through those days, she'd had to push everything else to the back of her mind.

But after she'd seen the casket lowered into the grave and returned to her job as a guidance counselor in the Dallas public school system, questions had invaded her daily thoughts, demanding answers.

Without concrete evidence, she would never believe her father had been drinking. George Backus had been a recovering alcoholic who hadn't had a drink in more than fifteen years. He'd joined Alcoholics Anonymous a few months after her mother's death, and from that day on had poured all his time and energy into his job and raising his daughter.

Molly had spent most of her summers in oil-field towns, from Texas to Alaska. During the school year, if her father's job took him away from home, she stayed with a great-aunt, who had died when Molly was a student at the University of Texas.

Although George Backus had been semiretired at the time of his death, he'd remained active as a free-lance geologist, taking occasional jobs that didn't require his traveling too far from home. He'd been excited about the job for Delaney Drilling, since another company had already brought in two good producers in the area. And he'd been happy to be working again after several months spent golfing and making repairs to his home in Dallas.

He'd gone to Sunset in late February, and his weekly letters to Molly had been both cheerful and optimistic. The letters came as regularly as clockwork, and Molly felt that wouldn't have been true if her father had started drinking again. Furthermore, they had contained no hint of depression or any other problems. Except for the last letter, written the day before he died.

Molly reached into the side pocket of her purse and pulled out that much-fingered and reread letter. Though she practically had it memorized, she unfolded it.

Dear Lala, it began. The salutation brought an ache to Molly's throat. As a toddler trying to say "Molly," the best she'd been able to manage was "Lala." That had delighted her father, and he'd never called her anything else.

Quickly, she scanned the first page. Her father had written of his plans for her visit in July. He'd been quizzing the locals about the best fishing holes, and had arranged to rent a boat and water-ski equipment for outings on the lake. He'd arranged for Molly to stay in the room next to his at the motel. The tool pusher who was occupying the room had generously offered it, agreeing to bunk with his brother while George's daughter was in town.

You'll like Jude Hammond, he'd written. *She owns the motel and adjoining restaurant. Her daughter, Lauren, is a little sweetheart, too.*

The final sentences on the last page struck the only odd note. Molly had puzzled over them repeatedly, trying to wring more meaning from them. *The prospects for this well are looking very good,* she read for what was at least the hundredth time, *but I'm starting to feel a strange undercurrent here. I'm beginning to suspect the Delaneys are up to something.*

That was all. No hint in that letter, or any of the previous ones, of what the "strange undercurrent" might be or what he suspected the Delaneys were "up to." Again Molly received no new flash of insight as to what her father had meant. Yet these few puzzling lines had hardened her suspicion that there was more to her father's death than the official verdict. Except for those last words, she might have convinced herself that her reluctance to accept the accidental death verdict was simple psychological denial. But by the time her two-month summer vacation had begun, she'd known she had to come to Sunset and find out for herself.

Now that she'd arrived, where did she begin? And how could she go around asking questions about George Backus's death without arousing suspicion? And that was the last thing she wanted to do, if her father's death hadn't been accidental.

Deep in thought, she didn't see the bald man approaching her car until he tapped on the window. She started so violently she thought her heart would leap out of her throat. Recovering with a shaky laugh, she rolled down the window.

"Are you having a problem, miss?"

"Oh, no. No, thank you. I'm just wondering where I might get a glass of iced tea and a burger."

"Jude Hammond's restaurant is the best in town. Use the motel entrance."

"Thank you again." She reached for the gearshift, eased it toward her and drove away.

After following an S-curve in the highway, she had a clear view of the town's business section. Sunset's short, dusty main street was bordered by wide sidewalks and well-maintained brick and rough-cedar business buildings. There was a single stoplight at the intersection of Main and Second. As Molly turned left on the green, she saw the black-on-white sign at the far end of the block. Hammond Motel and Restaurant had been painted on it in big, square letters.

The motel and restaurant occupied an L-shaped brick building with gray shutters. A covered drive marked the entrance. Molly found a vacant parking place and sat for a moment, gathering her thoughts.

She would go in for a burger and, if they had a vacancy, she would take it for a couple of nights. If she needed to stay longer, she would come up with a logical reason, in case anyone asked.

She stepped out of the car and tried to smooth out the worst wrinkles in her dress. Then she crossed the paved parking area to the restaurant. A sign in the window read Waitress Wanted. A second notice said Motel Office Inside. A third invited her to Come In.

She stepped into the dim, pleasant coolness of a tile-floored lobby. There was no one in the restaurant dining room off the lobby, but she heard muffled sounds coming from what had to be the kitchen beyond. She hesitated, looking around curiously. There was a No Vacancy sign on the cash register counter, which made her heart sink. But maybe somebody would check out today, she told herself.

In addition to the counter, a small walnut secretary sat against one wall with a guest book lying open on it. It added a homey touch to the place.

Molly walked over to the secretary. The page to which the book was open was half filled with names. "George Backus" was at the top, and Molly's throat tightened as she recognized her father's handwriting. She wrenched her gaze from the familiar scrawl and ran it over the names below her father's. The last name riveted her attention. Chet Delaney.

The troublesome words from her father's last letter leaped into her mind.

I'm beginning to suspect the Delaneys are up to something.

Her father had once told her that Delaney Drilling had begun as a partnership of two brothers. When one of the brothers died, his son came into the business as a half owner. Chet Delaney had to be either that son or his uncle. The realization brought a flutter of anxiety to Molly's stomach. She ignored it. She had to meet this Chet Delaney, get to know him, get him to trust her....

She heard footsteps approaching and quickly turned away from the guest book. A handsome, auburn-haired woman wearing a white, bibbed apron over a blue-and-white striped chambray dress came into the foyer from the dining room. Seeing Molly, she halted abruptly.

"Sorry to keep you waiting. I didn't hear you come in."

"That's all right. I just arrived."

A hopeful expression lit the woman's hazel eyes. "Tell me you've come about the waitress job." She clasped her hands together in mock prayer. "Please."

Taken aback by the woman's assumption, Molly hesitated. Then she decided to accept the gift fate offered. She smiled. "Well, yes. I, uh, saw your sign."

"Thank God! My best waitress and her boyfriend took off for California last week with less than an hour's notice. The other one broke her hip and will be out of commission for at least six weeks. I've been working myself to death around here ever since." She extended a hand. "I'm Jude Hammond. I own this place."

Molly accepted the hand. "Molly Sinclair."

"New in town?"

"Yes...I was only driving through, actually. I stopped at a filling station outside town and asked where I could get a burger. The man directed me here. Then I saw your sign and, well, I had no particular destination in mind, and I could use a job."

Jude Hammond cocked her head, studying Molly curiously. "Have you had any experience as a waitress?"

"Some." Molly had waited tables in an Arizona resort during one of her summer vacations in her college days. "It was a few years ago, so I may be rusty at first."

The woman breathed a sigh of relief. "It'll come back to you fast. I don't suppose you could start this afternoon, about five? That's when people begin coming in for dinner."

"I don't know. I have to find a place to stay and take a shower and . . ."

"Oh, I forgot to mention, a room and meals come with the job. I'd better warn you, though, it's not much of a room. Just enough space for a twin bed and a chest. I converted it from a storage closet for the last waitress. Added a little bathroom and closet at the back. It seemed the only way I could keep a good waitress for any length of time."

"It sounds fine." Better than fine, Molly was thinking. Living in the same motel with Chet Delaney meant she could find opportunities to talk to him. As the new waitress, she would arouse no suspicions, provided she could be patient and let Delaney get used to her being around before she started dropping questions about George Backus into the conversation. Patience had never been one of her virtues, but she would get the knack of it. This was too important to botch.

"You've saved my life, honey. Come on back to the kitchen and I'll get Elsie to fix you the best hamburger you ever sank your teeth into."

Molly smothered a twinge of guilt at Jude Hammond's relief at having found a waitress. Even room and board would not keep Molly in Sunset for more than a few weeks.

Elsie was Elsie Pelcher, "chief cook and bottle washer." She was a stick-thin woman in her fifties, with graying brown hair in a thick braid coiled atop her head. She nodded gravely when Jude introduced her, eyeing Molly's slight frame with skepticism, as though to say Molly didn't look strong enough to handle the hard work that would be required of her.

Molly also met Ingrid Meeker, the cashier, who was taking a break. Ingrid was young, blond and rather pretty. As soon as they were introduced, Ingrid looked Molly over like a judge toting up points at a dog show. Molly had seen that look before. Some women unconsciously took a competitive stance with every other female around.

Perhaps in an effort to put some flesh on Molly, Elsie served her a fat, oversized burger with crispy lettuce, sweet ripe tomato slices and a generous slathering of mayonnaise, along with fries and a giant glass of iced tea. Elsie then returned to her preparations for the evening meal, moving silently from stove to refrigerator to pantry.

"My daughter, Lauren, and I have an apartment at the far end of the motel," Jude was saying. She sat across from Molly at the kitchen table with a cup of coffee. "She's eight. I've been divorced since she was a baby."

"I see." Molly didn't know what else to say. But Jude Hammond went on without encouragement.

"We don't see much of her father. He lives in Santa Fe." She seemed lost in pensive thought for a moment as she sipped her coffee.

"Lauren's at a friend's house," Jude continued. "She's spending the night there, but you'll meet her tomorrow." She shook her head, as though to scatter old memories. A sprinkling of silver hairs among the auburn glinted with the movement. "The motel's small. Only five rooms, not counting yours."

Molly ate a bite of the delicious burger and took a drink of tea before she said, "I guess, in the motel business, you have a lot of turnover."

"Not lately. All the rooms are occupied by oil-field workers now. Four of them have been here since February, the other one since April." The April guest would have to be Chet Delaney, Molly thought, since his name was the last in the guest book. "Breakfast is included with the room rate," Jude continued, "and, believe me, the guests get their money's worth."

Elsie snorted an agreement from the pantry.

"I gather you serve all three meals in the restaurant," Molly said.

Jude nodded. "Except on Sundays when we only offer a buffet brunch from ten to two. I prepare the brunch with the help of a local housewife so Elsie can have Sundays off. You'll get Sunday off, too. The housewife's two daughters come along to serve drinks and clear tables. The other six days, I can handle the tables alone at breakfast, since it's buffet-style."

"When's your time off?" Molly asked.

Jude laughed shortly. "Between 10:00 p.m. and 6 a.m., unless I have bookkeeping to catch up on. Until Mae gets her cast off, you and I will have to cope with lunch and dinner by our lonesome. You'll work about three hours at lunch. Dinner is our busiest meal, but you'll have a couple of hours free between lunch and dinner. I realize it's not the best work schedule, but it's the nature of the business."

"It sounds okay. I don't have any place to go on my time off, anyway."

Curiosity flickered in Jude's eyes. "Where are you from?"

"The last place I lived was Dallas." Molly munched a French fry, then added, "I'm divorced, with no close family. I guess I needed a change."

Jude nodded in understanding, evidently assuming the divorce was recent. Molly didn't correct the false deduction, since it lent credence to her claim of "needing a change." If Jude asked her how long it had been, she wouldn't lie, but, with any luck, Jude wouldn't ask.

Molly finished the burger, and Jude said, "If you want to get your things, I'll show you the room." Molly went out to the car for her suitcase, then followed Jude down the hall leading off the foyer. A man stepped out of one of the rooms as they approached. He was of medium height, muscularly fit, with short, dark hair and boyish features, even though Molly judged him to be in his mid-thirties.

"Just getting up, David?" Jude asked.

"Yes, ma'am." His eyes strayed to Molly.

"This is Molly Sinclair, the new waitress," Jude said. "Molly, David Formby. He works the night tower as a tool pusher."

Molly remembered to look puzzled, as though she didn't understand oil-field jargon. "I'm working for Delaney Drilling as foreman on the night shift," David explained.

"Oh, I see."

"Well . . ." He shifted uncertainly. "Good to meet you, Molly."

"You, too," she said, smiling, and followed Jude to the end of the hall, where it angled to the right. Jude unlocked a door, then handed Molly the key.

"I don't think he liked me," Molly remarked as Jude pushed the door open.

"David's just shy," Jude said. "His brother Wilson's another story. Wilson's the tool pusher on the day tower. An outrageous flirt, that one, so be warned." She gestured with her thumb over her shoulder. "My apartment is around the corner." She led the way into the bedroom. "I told you it's not much," she said apologetically.

The room was about eight feet wide and ten feet long. A narrow brass bed was pushed against a small bedside table, which hugged the wall. A braided rag rug made a bright-colored puddle on the pine floor beside the bed. A four-drawer maple chest and a small, oak rocker with a patchwork pillow seat were the only other furnishings. Next to the head of the bed was a narrow window, its white miniblind transforming the light of the western sun into narrow stripes on the ceiling. The bathroom contained the necessary fixtures, including a stall shower. The closet was small, but adequate for Molly's needs.

"I like it," Molly said.

"Hardly enough room to skin a cat," Jude said with a smile. "But then I don't guess you'll be skinning many cats."

Molly put her suitcase on the bed and opened it. Realizing that Jude Hammond hadn't left, she looked over her shoulder. "Is there anything else?"

Jude's eyes narrowed in thought. "You haven't asked about the salary. Don't you want to know what the job pays?"

She'd slipped up there, Molly realized, and cautioned herself to be more careful in the future. "I assumed it would be minimum wage, since you're providing room and board.''

Jude named an hourly wage a little above the minimum and Molly said, "Good enough. I don't have any debts, so I don't need much." She hoped that would satisfy Jude's curiosity or at least postpone it for a while. "I'll come to the restaurant a little before five." Until then, she wanted to be alone to settle in.

"Well, I'll leave you to your own devices." Jude still hesitated. "If this evening is too soon for you . . . ?"

"It isn't. I'll be a new woman as soon as I shower and change."

After Jude left, Molly unpacked quickly, hanging the few casual clothes she'd brought in the closet. She set her sneakers, canvas walking shoes and leather sandals on the closet shelf and put her travel alarm clock on top of the chest, then arranged everything else in the drawers. Her suitcase slid easily out of sight beneath the bed. It took about five minutes, which left an hour and a half before she started work.

After a shower and shampoo, she lay on the bed in her underwear and watched the strips of sunlight drift westward across the ceiling. The motel was quiet, sleepy, like the town. It was hard to imagine anything violent happening there. But if her father's death hadn't been an accident, then it had been arranged somehow, by someone. But who? And why? As she lay there in the silence, her suspicions seemed a bit ridiculous, even to herself.

David Formby and another oil-field hand who, Molly soon learned, was employed as a roughneck, appeared for dinner on the stroke of five. When she went to take their orders, David introduced her to the other man, Larry Browning. He looked to be about nineteen and seemed even shyer than David.

The next hour and a half passed in a blur. The tables filled up quickly, and there was usually someone waiting to take a table as soon as it was vacated and cleared. She and Jude were kept so busy that she found herself practically running from the dining room to the kitchen to place and pick up orders. Finally Jude said, "If you don't slow down, girl, you'll collapse before closing time."

"When's that?" Molly asked breathlessly.

"Nine o'clock, but by the time the lingerers leave and we clear all the tables, it'll be nine-thirty or ten. So relax, okay? You're doing fine."

"Okay." Molly took a deep breath and went back to work. David and Larry left for the well site carrying lunch buckets packed by Elsie with sandwiches, chips, fruit, thermoses of iced tea and big triangles of apple pie.

The three other motel guests, who worked the day shift, appeared at six-fifteen. Molly caught only a glimpse of their backs in the foyer as they headed down the hall to their rooms to clean up for dinner. One of them, she knew, was Chet Delaney. She would meet him soon, and she began schooling her expression to reveal nothing but politeness when they came face-to-face.

To get the moment over with, she rushed to their table as soon as they sat down, before Jude could get there ahead of her.

"Hi." The dark-haired one greeted her with laughing brown eyes and an extended hand. "I'm Wilson

Formby. When my brother came to the site to relieve me, he told me Jude hired a new waitress. You're Molly, right?'' She could see the resemblance to his brother. Features that in David seemed boyishly half formed had a chiseled hardness in Wilson's face. He was handsome and clearly knew it. An outrageous flirt, Jude had said.

Molly flipped open her order pad to a fresh sheet. ''What'll it be?''

Wilson ignored the question. ''You're a lot better looking than Shirley.'' Evidently Shirley was the former waitress who'd gone to California with her boyfriend. ''Don't you think so?'' Wilson aimed a playful punch at the arm of the painfully thin young man on his right. ''This is Boney Armbruister.''

Boney looked no older than Larry, the night-tower roughneck. His sundarkened skin turned a deep red as he mumbled ''Hello'' in Molly's direction and ducked his head.

Wilson laughed. ''And this is one of my bosses, Chet Delaney.''

Molly had been carefully avoiding the third man's gaze, but now she braced herself to meet it. She found herself staring into a pair of penetrating blue eyes that seemed to fill her field of vision. With an effort, she pulled her eyes from the grip of his and let them skim quickly over the rest of him.

Like the other two, he was deeply tanned. Blond hairs dusted his arms. His hair was the sun-streaked straw blond that she'd seen on the last man going down the hall a half hour earlier. He was the tallest of the three, a shade over six feet, she guessed, from the glimpse she'd had of him in the foyer. His broad shoulders seemed to strain against the white knit fabric of his shirt. She judged him to be in his early thirties. Too young to be one of the original partners in Delaney Drilling. He had to be the nephew.

His hair was cut short, and one shower-damp lock fell across his forehead. The sun had etched squint lines at the corners of his blue eyes. He had an angular face, with faintly hollow cheeks beneath prominent cheekbones. His chin was squarish, with a shadowed cleft, his mouth lifted slightly at one corner in a speculative smile. He wasn't handsome in the classical sense, the way Wilson Formby was, but he was intriguing in an odd way. As though there were complicated depths to his character. Wilson struck her as being simpler; what you saw was exactly what you got.

Folding her arms across her breasts in an unconscious gesture of self-protection, Molly said, "Hello, Mr. Delaney. Are you ready to order?"

He held her gaze for an instant, and the lifted corner of his mouth rose fractionally higher, exposing even white teeth. Molly had the ridiculous feeling that he found her amusing. She wondered if she had a streak of dirt on her face, or lipstick on her teeth.

"I'll take the chicken fried steak with a baked potato and iced tea."

Molly bent over her pad, glad to finally have somewhere else to look, and scribbled the three orders. As she walked away, she heard Wilson Formby laugh and mutter something in a low tone to the others.

Molly didn't fully relax again until after Chet Delaney and the men with him left their table. She worked on steadily until the restaurant closed and the last table had been cleared, after which she went to the kitchen, poured herself a big mug of hot coffee and dropped into a chair.

Ingrid came in to say good-night. She hitched one hip up to rest against the door frame and ran scarlet-nailed fingers through her long blond hair. A small diamond glittered on the third finger of her left hand, Molly noticed.

"How was it?" Ingrid asked.

"A little hectic," Molly admitted.

Ingrid nodded absently, as though she wasn't really interested in Molly's answer. She'd merely been making conversation. Ingrid was self-absorbed, Molly realized. She would pay close attention to another woman only if she perceived the woman as a threat of some sort.

"See you all tomorrow," Ingrid murmured as she left.

"'Night, Ingrid," Jude muttered. She was loading the last of the dishes into the commercial-sized dishwasher, and Elsie was running a damp cloth over the range and cabinet tops.

Elsie glanced at Molly and said consolingly, "The first day's the hardest." From her tone, Molly guessed her uncomplaining performance had earned Elsie's admiration. Good. She needed all the friends here she could get.

"Exactly what I was telling myself," Molly agreed. "Are you always so busy?"

"We have been most nights since they started drilling west of town," Jude put in. "The other two motels are full of oil-field hands, too, and most of them come here for meals. And we've always done a steady trade with the locals. But I'm not complaining. It pays the mortgage.''

Elsie went to the pantry and came back with a black purse. ''I'm off, then.''

Jude and Molly bade her goodbye. Then Jude said, ''I'm going to work on the books. As for you, you'd better hit the sack.''

''In a few minutes,'' Molly said. After Jude left, she sat in the silent kitchen, listening to the quiet humming of the electric wall clock. Propping her elbows on the table, she slowly savored her coffee and tried to gather enough energy to get up and go to her room. She had forgotten how bone wearying it was, being on your feet five hours without a break.

More than anything, she wanted to put her head down on the table and close her eyes for a few minutes, but she restrained herself, fearing she'd fall asleep.

''Any coffee left in the pot?''

Molly turned her head sharply at the sound of the male voice. Chet Delaney was lounging in the kitchen doorway, his thumbs hooked over low-riding jeans. She blinked the drowsiness from her eyes. ''I think so.''

He crossed to the range and picked up the big stainless steel percolator to shake it. ''Sounds like about a cup. It's still hot, too.'' He took down a mug, filled it and brought it to the table. ''You look done in.''

She smiled wanly, knowing she'd chewed off her lipstick long ago and that her nose must be shining. Not that it mattered, really. ''Let me put it this way. I'll have no trouble sleeping tonight.''

He chuckled, and she concentrated on gathering her tired wits so that she could start getting acquainted with

Chet Delaney. "I haven't done this kind of work in a while. I worked in an office before."

"Why did you come to Sunset? Do you have family here?"

She studied him. Was there hidden knowledge behind the question? No, she told herself, he couldn't know who she was. "No." She shrugged. "Maybe I have itchy feet. Besides, I was tired of city traffic. I wasn't crazy about my job, either."

"What city?"

"Dallas. I was there several years, but I don't have any family left, so there was no regret in leaving." She fingered the handle of her mug, thinking that she'd better stop his questions with a few of her own. "Wilson Formby said you're his boss. Do you work the same shift?"

"The hands are on ten- to twelve-hour towers," he said. "I usually put in eight or nine hours. I'm the geologist on the well we recently started drilling."

A geologist. He was doing the job her father probably would have had, had he lived, and was sleeping in the room that had been her father's. "Is this the first well you've drilled around here?"

He shook his head. "The second. We had high hopes for the first—another company already brought in two producers in the Sunset field—but ours was a dry hole. I wasn't the geologist on that one. I was tied up on a well in the eastern part of the state."

"The other geologist picked the wrong spot?"

Molly tried to say it offhandedly, but some of her tenseness must have shown, because he looked at her carefully before he responded, and she dropped her eyes to stare into her half-full mug.

"Backus was a seasoned man. I'd probably have picked the same site he chose."

"Was?"

"He was killed in a car accident."

"Oh." Unaccountably, Molly's heart speeded up. Was she showing too much interest in a man she had supposedly never met? But it was too convenient an opportunity to pass up. "Did it happen in Sunset?" she asked carefully.

"About a half mile west of town. He lost control of his car and went into Sunset Lake. He'd just left the well site. He'd been drinking on the job." He said it matter-of-factly.

She darted a quick glance at him. He was sitting half-sideways in his chair, one arm flung over the high back, which appeared to stretch the knit shirt to its limit. There was something wild and reckless in this man, she thought. He seemed the epitome of the Texas wildcatter. She looked back into her cup. "I see." She didn't trust her voice beyond the two words. She forced back another question, intending to wait out the silence.

Finally the stillness became worse than speaking and she asked, "Had that been a problem before? The geologist drinking on the job, I mean."

He shook his head. "I hadn't known Backus long, but I liked him. I'd finished at the other site shortly before the accident. My Uncle Dirk and I had been in Sunset a couple of days, checking things out—we're partners in the drilling company. Backus had sent us reports of promising soil samples, and we hoped the men were about to hit pay dirt."

Molly lifted her eyes to his. "But you said it was a dry hole."

He nodded. "We found Backus's last report in the trailer at the site, after he died. The traces of oil had played out. He recommended plugging the hole, and we took his recommendation and looked for another site. Half of success in this business is knowing when to take your losses and move on." He brought his mug to his lips and added musingly, "Backus's reports were precise and thorough. I'd never have pegged him for a drunk. But we found a half full bottle of whiskey in the trailer where he worked, and the hands said he was staggering when he left the site to drive to town that day. They couldn't stop him."

His words pelted Molly like bruising stones, and she had an irrational impulse to cover her head with her arms to ward them off. *Lies!* she cried silently, clutching her mug so tightly that her fingers hurt. Suffering in silence was contrary to her nature, and it was all she could do not to blurt out a denial. She bit her bottom lip to keep the words from erupting. But she couldn't sit there another minute and listen to Chet Delaney slandering her father. If she did, she knew she would say something and give herself away.

Her anger gave her a spurt of energy that she used to shove back her chair and rise to her feet. "I'm going to fall asleep right here if I stay any longer," she said through stiff lips. "Good night." She turned away before he had a chance to say more than good-night in return. But she felt his gaze boring into her rigid back as she set her empty mug in the sink and left the kitchen.

Chapter 2

Exhausted as she was, Molly was too disturbed by her talk with Chet Delaney to fall asleep as soon as her head hit the pillow. Instead, her mind replayed the conversation in the kitchen until she wanted to scream.

We found a half full bottle of whiskey in the trailer.
He'd been drinking on the job.
I'd never have pegged him for a drunk.
He was staggering when he left the site.
They couldn't stop him.

She got up once and adjusted the window blind to keep a streetlight from shining in her eyes, again for a drink of water, and a third time to see if she'd set her alarm. She wasn't expected for work until eleven, but she wanted to get better acquainted with the town before then.

Finally she punched her pillow into a ball and lay down again. Once she heard a man's footsteps in the hall and wondered if they were Chet Delaney's. He'd talked about her father with seeming ease, as though he didn't question the accidental death verdict. As though he had nothing to hide. Yet her father's last letter indicated otherwise.

Even though she'd been looking for signs of evasion in Chet, she hadn't seen them. If the Delaneys had indeed been, perhaps still were, "up to something," Chet must be very confident that it wouldn't come to light now that George Backus was dead.

If only her father had been more specific about his suspicions. Then she would at least have an idea of what she was looking for. As it was, she was floundering around in the dark. And every time Chet Delaney looked at her, she had the feeling he knew it.

Which was absurd. The feeling came from her own anxiety and self-consciousness. She feared that somehow Chet Delaney and everyone else at the Hammond Motel would find out who she really was. If that happened, her chances of learning the truth about her father's death would be almost nonexistent.

When she closed her eyes, she saw Chet Delaney's narrowed, intelligent blue gaze assessing her. Wondering. Speculating. She saw the slight upturned corner of his mouth, as though his speculations amused him. Under other circumstances, she would have found him extremely attractive. But in her situation, she couldn't afford to see him as anything but a source of information, a source that she would have to cultivate with the utmost caution.

What if he already suspected that she was George Backus's daughter? Would he do something to stop her delving into the circumstances surrounding her father's death?

Would her own car end up in Sunset Lake?

Molly's sharp intake of breath hissed in the dark silence. She hadn't admitted it to herself before, but now she had to examine the possibility that her investigation might put her in danger. She flopped over on her back to stare at the faint lines of light around the miniblind. Stop it, Molly, she ordered herself. A few more leaps to melodramatic conclusions and her imagination would be so out of control that she wouldn't sleep at all.

If she was to accomplish what she'd come to Sunset for, she must proceed with judgment and common sense. Her father's vaguely phrased suspicion about the Delaneys didn't prove anything. He could have been wrong.

Even if he'd been right, the chicanery he'd alluded to in his last letter might be something relatively innocuous, like, well, like adding a little padding to tax-deductible business expenses. Or...

Molly couldn't think of another example at the moment, but there had to be plenty of questionable activities the owners of Delaney Drilling could be involved in that they wouldn't want known, activities serious enough to elicit a penalty from the IRS or a fine from some other governmental agency. But certainly not so serious that fear of exposure could lead to a man's death.

There were other possibilities, as well. Whether her father had been right or wrong about the Delaneys, his suspicions could have had nothing whatsoever to do with his death. He could have been drunk, as everyone said. Molly didn't believe it, but she couldn't exclude the possibility altogether. Or he could have been sober, but ill, perhaps staggering from light-headedness. He could have been merely tired; perhaps he'd been fighting sleep on that drive from the well site to town and had lost the battle on the stretch of road bordering the lake.

Molly hoped that one of these latter possibilities turned out to be the true one. Illness or weariness—even drunkenness—would be so much easier to accept than the darker possibilities that were keeping her from sleep.

After finishing his coffee, Chet went for a long walk, an exercise that was bearable only at night these days. Daytime temperatures had been above one hundred degrees for two weeks. The trailer where he ran his tests at the well site was air-conditioned, as was the second trailer, or "doghouse," where the crew retreated between spurts of physical labor. He wondered how anyone had survived July and August days in the west Texas oil fields before the advent of air conditioning. There must have been plenty of maneuvering for assignment to the night shift.

He kept his long legs moving at a strolling pace. When he felt a trickle of sweat slide down the base of his spine, he realized he'd unconsciously picked up speed while his mind had wandered to his kitchen conversation with Molly Sinclair, and he slowed his steps.

There was something about Molly Sinclair that nettled him. Something that didn't quite ring true, but he couldn't put his finger on it.

She was lovely; there was no confusion in his mind on that score. If he hadn't been so sure that serious attachments were not for him, a natural beauty like her would have knocked him off his feet. Even knowing that, he had found himself fascinated by the sheen of her wild tumble of inky curls, the way her soot-lashed gray eyes seemed to fill her face, the way her shirt clung to her small breasts, the delicate structure of her body, which gave her such an air of fragility.

Fragility? Maybe that was the false note. As they'd talked in the kitchen, he'd sensed that within her slight, feminine frame beat the heart of a fighter. He was sure she'd bristled once or twice, though he hadn't known which of his harmless remarks had hit her wrong. Perhaps she read insults into every conversation. Or every man's?

She had itchy feet, she'd said. She hadn't liked working in an office. She had no family. Jude had told him that Molly was recently divorced, the final ingredient in her desire for a change. Okay, he could buy that.

What he couldn't understand was why a young, attractive woman accustomed to city life would go to such drastic lengths to effect that change. Molly Sinclair had chosen—on the spur of the moment, according to Jude—to live and work in an isolated, dead-end town where half the time the weather seemed designed to drive out the few hardy folks who continued to cling to the unforgiving land.

Chet's thoughts led him to a tentative, yet seemingly inescapable, conclusion. Molly Sinclair was running away from something.

Probably her ex-husband, he mused. The divorce statistics never hinted at the misery that lay behind the figures, he told himself bitterly, remembering the unhappy mess his parents and his Uncle Dirk had made of their marriages.

He sometimes thought searching for oil was a disease. The nomadic life-style of men like his father and uncle would strain the best of marriages. Aside from that, the very nature of dyed-in-the-wool independent oil men, wildcatters, made them difficult husbands. Wildcatters were gamblers at heart, willing to risk everything on a hole in the ground, knowing full well they would lose it all ninety percent of the time. Many women found such men exciting, but few were equipped to deal with them on a permanent basis.

Marriage was a crap shoot under the best of circumstances. Chet had concluded long ago that there was no vine-covered cottage, no patter of little feet, in his foreseeable future. For him, it was the only sane conclusion. He spent over half his time in the field, sleeping in motels, eating in restaurants. Lately, however, the idea of giving up his nomadic existence for a more settled life no longer filled Chet with restlessness.

Recently a Houston-based conglomerate had been making discreet inquiries about Delaney Drilling, but Chet couldn't imagine his uncle agreeing to sell. On paper, he owned half the company, but his father and Uncle Dirk had started it on a shoestring and, as far as Chet was concerned, any decision to dispose of all or part of its assets was Dirk's. He was sure it would take something more than the company's current financial bind to push Dirk into relinquishing control.

He understood and accepted his uncle's desire to keep the company independent, a family concern, even though it meant his rootless existence would continue. He was so used to it that it was hard to imagine a change, his recent wishful thinking notwithstanding. The life still suited him well enough. He'd always been a loner. Lately, though, he'd been aware of an undertone of dissatisfaction without understanding its source. Probably this town, he told himself.

The problem with Sunset, he thought morosely, was that there was nothing to do except work. Add that to living in one room where the walls sometimes threatened to squeeze the breath out of you, and you had a recipe for frustration. If you wanted an evening out, you could choose one of three dreary bars or the movie house where the film changed once a week.

The four other men staying at the Hammond Motel were in the same predicament. Add an attractive new woman like Molly Sinclair to the mix, and you were asking for trouble. Hell, maybe that was all there was behind his unsettled feelings about the new waitress. She was beautiful, and he was lonely and frustrated— a man who hadn't had a woman in too long. A man who, if he had any sense at all, would keep a safe distance between himself and Molly.

He knew somehow that Molly wasn't the kind of woman with whom he could let down his emotional guards. But there were always plenty of that kind around, the ones who wanted nothing but a roll in the sack and a few laughs. Maybe it was time he looked for one. Somehow the thought didn't lessen his feeling of frustration.

He walked a very long time before he returned to his room that night.

The next morning Molly wandered down Main Street, stopping at the drugstore and the jewelry store, where an interesting array of turquoise pendants and earrings filled the display window. She went inside and lingered over the display, trying on several necklaces and engaging the clerk in conversation.

After a few minutes Molly remarked casually, "I'm new in town."

"I didn't think I'd seen you before," said the young woman. "I'm Jill Rice."

"Molly Sinclair. I'm working as a waitress for Jude Hammond."

"You must have taken Shirley's place."

Molly nodded and said confidingly, "I think Jude's pretty put out with Shirley. Apparently she left without giving notice."

The young woman grinned. "That's Shirley for you. I was in her high school class. You never knew what she would do next."

Molly lifted a dangling silver-and-turquoise feather earring to her ear, turning her head to admire her reflection in the small mirror resting on the counter. "Lucky for me, she decided to trade in her job for California."

"You're not married?"

"Uh-uh." Molly returned the earring to the velvet case. "Not anymore."

The clerk looked sympathetic. "You won't get too lonely over at Jude's place. She has all those single men staying with her. Have you met Wilson Formby yet?"

"I've met them all."

"Isn't Wilson *cute?*"

"He's all right. I— Well, I guess I've had my fill of young men," Molly improvised quickly. "I'd like to meet someone older, more settled. I think there was an older man staying at Jude's before I arrived."

"Oh, that's the geologist who drowned in Sunset Lake. He had a weird name. Backup, or something. You wouldn't have been interested in him. He was *really* old. In his sixties, probably."

"Did you know him?"

"Never met him. I ran into Wilson and some of the others at Dewey's Lounge a few times, but the geologist wasn't with them. Not very sociable, I guess."

"Hmm. Well, thanks for showing me the jewelry." There was nothing to be learned about her father here, Molly thought, except that he hadn't frequented Sunset's bars. This seemed to bolster her conviction that he hadn't started drinking again. At least, she thought reluctantly, not in public. "I'll think about the earrings," she added as she left.

"You can put them on layaway," the young woman called after her.

The clerk at the drugstore was too busy to engage in conversation, so Molly walked back to the motel, having accomplished nothing.

She went in for breakfast at ten, expecting to have the dining room to herself until it was time to start her lunch shift. Jude was removing the remains of the breakfast buffet, but Molly was in time to help herself to scrambled eggs, biscuits and coffee. She was already headed for a table against one wall when she saw

Chet Delaney sitting in the corner, drinking coffee and reading a newspaper.

He glanced up at her over the top of reading glasses that gave him a scholarly look, at odds with his deep tan and muscular body. He removed the glasses and tucked them in his shirt pocket. "Join me?"

She hesitated only fractionally before going to his table. "Aren't you working today?"

"I'm heading out in a while. I was waiting for a call from my office. I was afraid I'd miss it between here and the site. It came a few minutes ago, but I decided to read Jude's newspaper and have another cup of coffee before going out."

Molly split a warm biscuit and spread butter on it, uncomfortable with his keenly focused gaze. He had a way of looking at her that made her feel like a puzzle he was intent on solving. The July sunshine, only partly dimmed by unlined, muslin curtains, captured him in its brightness. His teeth glistened beneath a firmly sculptured upper lip. For an instant Molly wished that he was just another oil-field hand and not one of the suspect Delaneys.

"Setting your own hours is one of the advantages of being the boss," she murmured.

He nodded, his eyes never leaving her face. "Sometimes I think the advantages are outweighed by the other side of the scales."

"Really?" A note of faint disbelief crept into her voice. She lifted her chin. "Are you saying you'd rather be doing the dirty work for an hourly wage?"

Something indecipherable flickered in her eyes. Chet couldn't figure this woman out. If it weren't so unreasonable, he'd think she distrusted him, that she heartily disliked him. Not because he was a man and she was off men, but because he personally offended her. Yet she barely knew him, so it made no sense. There was no way to react except with good humor. He would eventually work out what made Molly Sinclair tick.

He looked at her with an amused crinkling of his eyes. "No, I didn't say that. I was merely commenting on the current depressed state of the oil business."

He recognized the flicker this time. It was sudden, intent interest, though he was baffled as to why his tossed-off remark should warrant it.

"Is Delaney Drilling in financial difficulties?"

Chet's laughter rang through the dining room like the clear peal of a bell. Molly watched him in astonishment. She had taken a risk by asking the impertinent question, seeing no other way to begin gathering the information that would help her. She had half expected indignation, perhaps outrage. Never humor. Yet seeing Chet Delaney laugh so unreservedly was like stumbling on a rare and precious piece of jewelry in a junk shop. Something you kept turning this way and that to study from different angles. Something you knew you had to have.

"Molly Sinclair," he said, teeth sparkling brilliantly as he leaned toward her, "I can't decide whether you're insultingly brash or totally without guile. You are a genuine mystery."

"That—that's ridiculous. If my question insulted you, I'm sorry."

"No you aren't." Chet continued to smile at her as though she were a child engaged in telling the most transparent of lies.

It was going to be more difficult than she'd imagined to get any hard facts from the man, Molly thought unhappily. "I *have* insulted you."

"What makes you think so?"

She ate the last bite of her biscuit and pressed her napkin to her mouth. "You haven't answered my question—the one about your financial difficulties," she pointed out.

"Supposed difficulties," he amended.

"But you're the one who suggested that owning Delaney Drilling has its disadvantages. You said the oil business was depressed."

"And you turned that into financial difficulties for Delaney Drilling. That's a leap in logic, wouldn't you say?"

She eyed him steadily. "Is it?"

Sitting back in his chair, he ran a hand over his face. "Tell me something, Molly. Why are you so interested in my company's financial status?"

Time to back off. "I'm not, really. *You* started us on this conversation. I was just trying to do my part. Forget it." She placed her napkin beside her plate. "You can be as secretive as you like. It doesn't matter to me. Now, I have to go to work."

"Secretive?" He said the word as though he were turning it over in his mind as he watched her rise and stack her dishes. "Well, then that makes two of us, doesn't it?" he asked, his tone low and thoughtful.

Molly picked up her dishes, as though she hadn't heard, and carried them to the kitchen.

Chet Delaney didn't miss much, she told herself, and she'd better not forget it. Oh, yes, this was going to be much harder than she'd imagined.

It would be twenty minutes before the dining room was open for lunch. Molly busied herself in the interim, helping Elsie in the kitchen. Jude had disappeared, probably taking a break in her apartment.

By the time Jude appeared at five of eleven, Chet had left the restaurant, presumably for the well site. "I have to go pick up Lauren in a few minutes," Jude said. "Molly, can you handle the dining room alone for a bit?"

"I'll give it my best shot."

Jude poured herself a cup of coffee. "Thanks." She blew on the surface of the coffee before taking a sip. "I've got a seven-dollar imbalance in the books that I have to find. And after lunch I have to take Lauren to the park and wait while she has her swimming lessons. One of my salesmen is due today, too, and I need to place a big order. The way my luck is going, he'll come while I'm at the park."

"I'll have some free time after lunch," Molly said. "Would you like me to take Lauren for her lesson?"

Jude gave her an assessing look. "Are you sure you wouldn't mind? You must have other things you'd like to do on your break."

"Can't think of a single one. Actually, I'm looking forward to meeting your daughter."

Jude's smile was grateful. "Okay, you asked for it. The lesson lasts forty-five minutes. I usually take something to read. There's a shelter with a cold drink machine where you can wait for her." She blew on her coffee again. "I'm going after Lauren now." She left, carrying her coffee cup with her.

* * *

Molly was taking an order when Jude returned twenty minutes later, accompanied by a skinny, red-haired, freckle-faced little girl carrying an overnight bag.

"Mama says you're taking me for my swimming lesson," Lauren stated, her green eyes taking Molly's measure.

"If it's all right with you," Molly said.

The green eyes measured her some more. "Okay. I have to be there at two-thirty."

"It only takes a couple of minutes to drive to the park," Jude said.

Lauren looked anxious. "If we're late, you won't be able to get a parking place in the shade."

"When do you think we should leave?" Molly asked the child. "Is two-fifteen early enough?"

Lauren's face cleared. "Yes."

"You'd better take a nap before then, young lady," Jude said. "Cassie's mother said you girls giggled all night."

"Oh, Mother," Lauren responded, rolling her eyes. "I'm not sleepy."

"Lie down for a little while anyway," Jude told her. "Now scoot."

Lauren sighed in resignation. "I'll meet you in the lobby, Molly."

Jude watched her daughter leave the kitchen, swinging the overnight case. "Summers are hard," she mused, half to herself. "I don't get to spend enough time with her."

Elsie lifted a wire basket full of French fried pota-
toes from a simmering vat of oil and deposited them on
a plate. "She misses Mr. Backus."

Molly jerked her head around. "Mr. Backus?"

"He stayed at the mótel a few months back," Elsie
said as she flipped a ground beef patty on the griddle.

"He worked for Delaney Drilling," Jude explained.
"He and Lauren hit it off from the first. George used
to take her fishing on his days off and to a movie once
in a while. He had a real knack with kids. Poor man
drank too much and drove his car into the lake. Lauren took it real hard."

"I remember now," Molly said. "Chet mentioned
it."

"I never saw George Backus drink," Jude said. "He
told me he'd been a member of Alcoholics Anonymous for years." She shook her head sadly. "He sure
seemed to have it all together. Last man in the world I'd
have expected to fall off the wagon."

"Just goes to show," Elsie observed. "You never can
tell about people. About the time you think you know
'em, they do something to shake you up."

"The last conversation I had with George," Jude
said, "he was telling me about his daughter coming to
visit him this summer, all excited about it." She glanced
toward the range. "What was it George called his
daughter, Elsie?"

"Lala," Elsie said without turning around. "It
must've been a nickname." She placed grilled ground
beef patties on buns lined up next to the range. "These
orders are ready to go, Molly."

Chapter 3

After the swimming lesson, Molly took Lauren to the drugstore for ice cream. They sat on high stools at the old-fashioned soda fountain.

"Your mother says you're quite a fisherman," Molly commented.

Lauren licked up a dollop of chocolate ice cream before it dripped off her cone. Her wet hair was tied back with a ribbon. Her freckled face was pink with sunburn, even though Molly had followed Jude's instructions and smeared every exposed inch of the child's skin with sunblock before her swimming lesson. "George taught me. I liked it when he took me fishing," Lauren said. She glanced at Molly. "George was nice."

Molly nodded companionably.

"He died."

"I heard."

"They said he was drunk, but I don't believe it." She ran the pink tip of her tongue delicately around the top of her cone, making the ice cream last.

Covertly, Molly studied Lauren's profile. "Why not?"

Lauren frowned and took a small bite of ice cream. "'Cause George hated whiskey and beer and all that stuff. He said it wasn't good for nothin' but to make trouble. He said it could make you hurt the people you love the most."

Molly had always known that her father blamed himself for her mother's death because he was sleeping off a drunk on the living room sofa the night she had her heart attack. By the time he'd awakened the next morning and stumbled into the bedroom, she'd been dead for hours. The doctor had said she'd probably died instantly, that he didn't think he himself could have saved her if he'd been there when it happened. Even so, Molly's father still blamed himself. She blinked the sting from her eyes and cleared her throat.

After a moment Lauren added, "One night David and Wilson were making lots of noise outside the motel, laughing and falling down." She made a face. "They woke me up. They were right outside my bedroom, and they were drunk. I was going to yell at them to shut up, but then I heard George. I guess they woke him up, too. He called them drunken idiots and said if they didn't pipe down he'd call the police."

Lauren looked over at Molly with a little frown creasing the pink skin between her sandy eyebrows. "George was real mad. And David called George a boring old tee-total-er." She pronounced the last word carefully. "I asked Mama what that was, and she said it was somebody who wouldn't even take a sip of any whiskey or beer or nothin' like that. So how could George have got drunk and wrecked his car?"

"I don't know," Molly replied. It was time to change the subject before Lauren—or Molly herself—started to cry. "You and I could go fishing sometime, if you'd like."

Lauren thought about it for a moment. "Okay. We could go to the lake. I can show you where the best place is to fish on the bank. I caught a three-pound catfish there."

"You have an extra pole?"

"You can use Mama's. She never has time to go fishing."

"How about next Sunday?"

Lauren grinned. "You mean it?"

"Sure."

"O-kaay!"

The dinner crowd that evening was smaller than the day before. Jude said it was because the Lions Club was having a banquet that night at the National Guard armory hall. Molly felt much more relaxed and competent as she went about her duties. At about seven o'clock, she saw Wilson Formby hanging over the cash register, flirting with Ingrid, who was laughing, clearly enjoying the attention. Then Wilson leaned closer and said something that made Ingrid blush.

Molly turned away to take care of a new customer. A few minutes later, Wilson sauntered into the restaurant with Chet Delaney, Boney Armbruister and two other oil-field workers who were staying at another

motel but who ate most of their meals at Jude's restaurant. They took the big round table in the corner.

Molly pushed through the kitchen's swinging doors,
carrying four chicken dinners for the young family
seated at a window booth. Glancing toward the corner
table, she caught Chet Delaney watching her with a
speculative expression that unsettled her. What she'd
give to be able to read minds! He caught her staring,
and she quickly looked away.

Jude was in the kitchen, and Molly took her time
serving the family in the booth and making sure they
had everything they wanted, giving Jude time to get to
the table in the corner, from where male laughter
erupted. But soon the four water glasses were filled, the
basket of bread and bowl of butter patties were in
place, and Jude still hadn't come out of the kitchen.

Ignoring the corner table any longer would look
strange. Molly gave herself a mental shake, reminding
herself that keeping the cautious distance from Chet
Delaney that feminine instinct dictated would not help
her learn what he knew about her father's death. She
picked up five menus and made her way to his table.

She passed out the menus, saying she'd be back in a
few minutes to take their orders. As she turned to go,
Wilson Formby deftly closed his hand around her
wrist. At her startled expression, he winked wickedly.
"Hey, don't run off so quick, Molly. You aren't that
busy."

Chet Delaney raised his menu and leaned back in his
chair, pretending to be contemplating his order, but
Molly was sure he didn't have to look at it. He must
have it memorized by now. The other three men ig-

nored their menus and watched Molly and Wilson with unabashed amusement.

Molly looked at the wrist that Wilson held, then met his eyes without responding to his smile. "Are you ready to order?" she inquired coolly.

Wilson dropped her wrist and looked almost, but not quite, sheepish. "What's good tonight?"

Recalling her conversation with Lauren at the drugstore soda fountain earlier that day, Molly wondered suddenly if Wilson remembered her father's threat to call the police the night he and David returned to the motel, noisily drunk. What had he and David thought of her father? she wondered. One of them must have been working at the well site the day her father staggered to his car and drove to his death. Had his coworkers really tried to stop him?

"Molly?" Wilson's questioning eyes told her she'd been staring at him too long. "You gonna tell us what's good tonight?"

The man was irrepressible. A smile tugged at the corner of her mouth. "Certainly not you, Wilson."

The audience broke into raucous laughter, and Molly even thought she heard a chuckle from behind Chet's menu.

"She's got your number already, Wilson," chortled Boney Ambruister.

"Aw, come on, Molly," Wilson wheedled in a husky voice that must have sent chills up dozens of female spines. "I know you really like me. There's a new film at the movie house tonight. Wanna go?"

"Gosh darn, Wilson," Molly replied, "I already made other plans."

"I thought you had a date with that Jill girl at the jewelry store tonight," said the man seated next to Wilson.

Wilson ignored him. "Tomorrow night, then?" he asked Molly.

She shook her head with mock regret. "Sorry. Can't make it."

Getting the message at last, Wilson lounged back in his chair, his eyes puzzled. Clearly he found it hard to believe that she could resist his practiced line. Was it really such a unique experience? Molly wondered, wanting to laugh aloud at the little-boy hurt in his mournful expression. She wanted an opportunity to get Wilson talking about her father, but not by accepting a date with him. That would encourage him to believe she wanted to be more than friends, and he didn't need any encouragement.

Wilson heaved an elaborate sigh. "Where did I go wrong?" he asked his companions. "She won't even tell me what to order."

"Try crow," Molly suggested sweetly as she walked away. The men with Wilson cracked up. Molly headed straight for the kitchen, returning to the corner table a few minutes later with a water pitcher.

Wilson squinted at her with narrowed eyes, as though trying to figure out what her game was. She gave him an impersonal smile and asked pleasantly, "What'll it be?"

"Give you three guesses," he quipped.

Molly just looked at him until he gave his order in an insolent drawl, then subsided into his chair while she turned her attention to the other men. Perhaps she imagined it, but she thought she detected a faint glimmer of approval in Chet's look as he ordered.

When Molly returned to the kitchen with the orders, Jude asked, "What did you say to our resident Romeo?"

"Pardon?"

"What were those guys laughing at?"

"Nothing much. Wilson asked me to go to a movie, and I turned him down."

"Good for you," Elsie said with approval. "That young man is too cocky by half. Needs taking down a notch or two."

"He's harmless," Molly said.

"As long as you don't take him seriously," Jude added. "Like some. He has Ingrid eating out of the palm of his hand."

"Isn't she engaged?" Molly asked.

"I never noticed that cramping Wilson's style much," Jude observed. "And Ingrid's as silly as a goose when it comes to good-looking men who whisper sweet nothings in her ear. I don't envy that poor boy she's planning to marry."

"If somebody more to her liking doesn't turn up," muttered Elsie.

"That isn't really any of our business, is it?" Jude asked of no one in particular.

If Ingrid was as inconstant as Jude seemed to think, Molly mused as she returned to work, her fiancé would be better off in the long run if the girl did find somebody else. Molly didn't think that somebody else would be Wilson Formby, though. Having known several men of Wilson's ilk in her time, she was sure he would sense the moment a woman began to expect more of him than he intended to give and back off in a hurry. It seemed clear to Molly that Wilson enjoyed charming women too much ever to be satisfied with confining that charm to a single member of the species.

As if to confirm Molly's opinion of him, Wilson left the motel less than an hour later, dressed in knife-pleated navy trousers, a snowy shirt and a flashy tie, whistling a cheery tune. He gave her a grin and a jaunty wave as he left, as though to say he harbored no ill feelings for her put-down in front of his cronies at dinner. Going to keep his date with Jill Rice, no doubt, Molly thought as she returned his wave good-naturedly.

By closing time at nine, there were no diners left in the restaurant and, within a few minutes, Jude and Molly had prepared the tables with fresh cloths and silverware for the next morning's breakfast. By nine-twenty Molly was unwinding beneath a warm, relaxing shower, enjoying the pleasant fantasy of retiring early with a good book. Unfortunately, she'd brought no books with her and hadn't thought to choose a paperback from the drugstore rack. If the store stayed open late, perhaps she could still buy a book tonight.

After stepping out of the shower, she dried herself quickly, then towel-dried and finger-combed her short curls. She threw on a clean pair of shorts and a knit shirt, and slid her bare feet into sandals.

She grabbed her car keys and a ten-dollar bill, then ran down the hall. She hesitated in the lobby, then decided to phone the drugstore before driving there. She listened to a dozen rings before replacing the receiver, disappointed. She should have known no business would stay open this late in Sunset. There wouldn't be enough trade to warrant it.

Sighing, she pocketed the money and keys and wandered outside to sit on the low bench near the entrance doors. Some of the day's heat lingered in the night air, but a slight breeze ruffled her damp curls, cooling her face and neck.

She rested the back of her head against the brick facade of the building, turning her face to take the best advantage of the breeze.

A few minutes later, she heard one of the lobby doors open. She looked around. Chet was standing there, one hand still holding the door ajar. He stared down at her.

"Hi," she said.

"Hi." He came over to stand beside her, propping one athletic shoe on the bench. He wore the same knit shirt and low-riding jeans he'd had on earlier in the restaurant, only now that he was standing so close, she was more aware of the way the much-washed denim hugged his lean, taut thighs and outlined his masculinity so faithfully. She felt her cheeks heat and jerked her gaze away. "Come out for a breath of fresh air?" he inquired.

"Yeah." She hoped he didn't notice the flustered catch in her voice. "I was going to the drugstore for a book, but it's closed."

"Everything closes at six except the bars, restaurants and the movie house—where you could be right now, watching a movie with Wilson Formby."

She gathered her scattered senses and focused them on his teasing tone, away from the heat generated in her face by the close proximity of such striking masculinity. "I think he took the girl from the jewelry store."

"You had your chance. With Wilson, you have to be quick. But I'm sure there will be other opportunities. Wilson doesn't hold a grudge."

She grinned. "Gee, what a relief." She tilted her chin to see his expression better. Half of his face was blurred by shadow. "You going out to the well?"

He shook his head. "For a walk. It helps me sleep."

He has trouble sleeping, she thought, and wondered why. A guilty conscience?

She was silent, occupied by the question, for the space of a heartbeat; then, before she could worry about what she was doing and change her mind, she blurted, "Could you stand some company?"

His silence lasted for two heartbeats, during which his gaze met Molly's. But his tone was casual when he replied, "Sure."

He seemed in no hurry, ambling along with easy strides, perhaps in deference to her shorter legs. Their route took them through a residential area of modest houses with lighted windows.

"Sunset must be a pretty dull place after Dallas," he observed when they'd walked a block without speaking. "You'd have to drive more than fifty miles to find any nightlife."

Molly lifted her face to the breeze. "This nightlife is enough for me." She felt his curious gaze on her but didn't acknowledge it until her arm accidentally grazed his. She jerked it away and met his eyes briefly to see if he thought she'd done it on purpose. God, what was wrong with her? What did it matter what he thought?

She wanted nothing from him except whatever he knew about her father's death.

He glanced down at his feet as they turned a corner. "Give it a couple of weeks. You'll be glad to go out with Wilson then."

"I doubt it."

"He's a good-looking man. Ingrid thinks he could be a film star. She told him he ought to go to Hollywood."

Why did he keep harping on Wilson Formby? "And take her with him, I presume."

"Probably." He looked over at her again, almost scowling. "Do you have something against Wilson?"

"No. I just don't think he'd wear well. All that charm is nothing but a game he plays, and any woman who thinks it's more than that will be the loser."

She had spoken with more emphasis than she'd intended and realized that she was comparing Wilson to her ex-husband. Tom had been incredibly handsome and charming, too. Only, when the honeymoon was over, she'd discovered there was nothing more to him than that. He had no depth. It was like eating cotton candy at every meal. Eventually you couldn't stand the sight of another cone of spun sugar.

With Tom, she learned that good looks and charm wear thin quickly in the face of a crisis. When he lost his job and couldn't find another, he grew surly and petulant, blaming Molly for "tricking" him into a marriage that he'd professed to want as much as she had.

"Wilson is like a cream puff," she went on musingly, thinking that she could easily have substituted her ex-husband's name. "Pretty and sweet and tempting on the outside, but without much substance on the inside.''

His lips curled lightly. "I'm surprised."

She looked up at him. He was peering down at her intensely, she sensed, though the expression in his eyes was hidden by the night. "Why?"

"You've just given an accurate thumbnail sketch of Wilson Formby on the basis of two days' casual acquaintance."

"Call me psychic," she said lightly.

"I'd rather think you speak from experience. You knew a man a lot like Wilson, knew him well and were badly hurt by him. Am I close?"

"It's uncanny."

"Your ex-husband?"

She shrugged and looked away from him. "There are some superficial similarities, I suppose." She found herself as surprised as Chet by the turn the conversation had taken. Yes, she had been hurt by the failure of her marriage, and humiliated by her own poor judgment in thinking Tom was somebody she could grow old with.

She and Tom had been college sweethearts, and she'd been the envy of half the girls on campus because of it. She had to admit that it had been gratifying to be the focus of so much attention, the girl Tom had chosen from all the others. But along with the hurt and humiliation, the gratification had disappeared long ago. She rarely even thought of Tom anymore. That period of her life was simply no longer important. On some subconscious level, Wilson Formby had stirred things she'd long ago put to rest.

"You're still in love with him." Chet's deep voice interrupted her thoughts.

"What?"

"Your ex-husband. You're still carrying a torch for him."

Her head came up. "That's not true!"

He said nothing for a moment, then went on, "You left Dallas to get away from the memories, didn't you?"

If she gave him an unequivocal, truthful no, she might have to explain why she had really left Dallas. She decided to let him think what he chose. She swallowed a denial and instead murmured noncommittally, "Mmm."

"At least you have the sense not to try to catch Wilson on the rebound."

Pushed to the point of rashness, she halted abruptly and planted her hands on her hips. "Catch Wilson! On the rebound!"

He stopped, too, unperturbed by her sputtering reaction. "I've seen it happen. For some reason, a lot of divorced people think another marriage is the answer to all their problems. It doesn't seem to occur to them that marriage *is* the problem."

Her eyes flared. "Boy, are you a cynic. Wait, don't tell me. You've had a bad marriage, too. Right?"

"Nope. Never even came close. I grew up with two miserable marriages. My parents' and my uncle's. My father and uncle were away from home a lot. My mother and aunt couldn't handle it. Come to think of it, I don't know many oil men whose marriages have endured. They make lousy husbands."

Molly felt her hackles rising. Was he still talking about Wilson Formby, or was he referring to himself now? Warning her off and telling her that he wasn't available, in case she had any idea about "catching him" on the rebound? What conceit!

"Maybe it's not their life-style that's to blame," she shot back angrily. "Maybe it's their colossal egos."

He uttered a bark of surprised laughter. Perhaps he didn't realize she was referring to him, she thought. But his next words proved otherwise. "So you think I'm egotistical," he said as he resumed walking, his tone implying that it mattered little to him.

The conversation was getting too personal. And it was serving no useful purpose. She was wasting an opportunity to learn something about her father. "Recklessly self-confident, anyway."

He threw her a bemused look. "What do you mean?"

"In spite of what you said the other night, I think Delaney Drilling desperately needs to bring in a producing oil well."

She expected him to challenge the statement. Instead he said, "You lost me. I don't see the connection."

"I'll bet the company's deeply in debt," she went on defiantly.

"We borrowed operating capital to drill the second well in the Sunset field," he admitted, "but debt is the name of the game in American business. It's what fuels the economy."

"But isn't it reckless to go back to the same field after you've just had a dry hole?"

"Not in this case," he said emphatically. "Remember, there are two producing wells in the field already. We know there's oil out there."

"You missed it the first time," she pointed out.

"Yeah, well, it happens. I've practically memorized the logs Backus used, and I still say he made an intelligent choice when he selected the drilling site. Apparently he just missed the outer edge of the pool. It can't happen again."

Molly laughed. "Obviously it can, and it has. Oil men think *every* wildcat well is a sure thing, when the truth is they have only one chance in ten of being right. They're the biggest gamblers in the world."

He jerked his head around and caught her upper arms, stopping her dead in her tracks. A thrill shot through her.

"How do you know so much about it?" he demanded.

The thrill, and the silly assumption that he was going to kiss her, disappeared. Once again, she'd talked too much. What was wrong with her? Her unthinking words would trip her up yet. What was it about this man that made her so careless? Brazen it out, Molly, she told herself.

She shrugged off his hands and took a step back. "I'm a Texan, remember? I'd have to be deaf and blind to live here and not have learned something about the oil business." He was still staring at her with doubt in the hard line of his jaw. "Besides," she added for good measure, "my ex-husband worked as a roughneck during college." Which was true, even if it was only for one summer and before she actually met him.

Chet continued to study her face. She wondered, with a frisson of alarm, if she was courting danger by imagining she could match wits with this man.

Though outwardly composed, Chet was also asking himself some hard questions. Why had he touched her? It had happened without his even thinking about it. In that first moment of feeling her fragile bones beneath his hands and knowing she was helpless, he had realized he should release her and walk away. But he hadn't.

Never before had he been so intent on figuring a woman out. It was crazy, but he had to know what made Molly tick. For some reason, he didn't believe she'd drifted into Sunset aimlessly. She simply didn't strike him as an aimless person. But he still didn't know why she had come. He wanted to know and, damn it, that angered him. He didn't want to be intrigued by her, and yet he was.

Frightened by her own thoughts and by the harshness in his face, Molly didn't trust herself to speak. Instead, she whirled and stalked away, back toward the motel. She had to get herself together before she risked talking to him again. She heard his footsteps behind her and walked faster, almost running.

She had reached an intersection when he caught up with her. His face, revealed in the light of the corner lamppost, was like a thundercloud. "What the hell is wrong with you?"

"Nothing!" she snapped.

"Watch it," he warned suddenly. "That's a steep curb."

But she had already stepped out, looking over her shoulder at him instead of where she was placing her foot. She landed wrong, her ankle twisting, and would have gone down if he hadn't reached her in time. He caught her, and she felt herself being lifted completely off the ground. Her legs went limp against his, and her head snapped back at his muttered, "Don't tell me there's nothing wrong, you little fool. What is it?"

"I'm not a fool...." His face was close to hers, his eyes blazing. Her words dwindled feebly. She had to admit she'd been behaving rather foolishly. "I'm sorry I invited myself on this walk. I thought we could be friends. But I don't like you. I think you're rude and conceited and—"

"Really?" Chet's brows came together in accusation. "I don't believe you, Molly."

All the strength had drained out of her body. She was a rag doll in his hands. A ghastly scene flashed through her mind. She lay in the street, helpless and broken, and he stood over her, saying that he knew who she was and why she'd come to Sunset, and that he was going to put a stop to her questions.

Chet, churning with sensations that bore no identifiable connection to the situation at hand, was unable to think clearly. When she had run away from him, fury had risen in him. She was afraid of him! It made no sense, but he could not deny the look she'd given him before she'd rushed off, the panicked look of a cornered deer. "You may not want to like me, but you do," he grated.

Her eyes flared, frightened but defiant. "Put me down."

Driven by an attraction he didn't understand, he crushed her roughly to him. Her body fit perfectly against his, her breasts soft against his chest. Her hair was a tangled, dark cloud around her pale face. The clean, soapy scent of her skin seduced him, and he felt the painful knife thrust of desire.

He didn't want to feel any of it. He hadn't intended for any of this to happen. His unreasoning anger and the deep, instinctive suspicion that she was playing a role, that her request to come walking with him was part of some complicated, feminine scheme, retreated. They were blurred by masculine admiration and an impotent craving to make love to her even while he knew it would be a disastrous mistake.

Insanely, he wanted to see those defiant gray eyes grow languid and glazed with feminine need. "Molly," he muttered, and his mouth blindly sought hers, found it, reveled in the hot taste of it for an instant, before she wrenched her head to one side and escaped the kiss.

She turned and twisted, struggling to breathe, pleading, "No, no." But she feared herself more than she feared him. With her body pressed against his, she knew that what she was feeling was pure primitive instinct too deep for understanding. Oh God, what was happening to her?

"You know you don't want to fight me," he muttered against her lips, his tongue probing gently.

Molly felt her insides melting, flowing toward him in hot surrender. She struggled against the feeling with a low cry. "Damn you."

Chet heard the despair in her voice and hated himself for his groping, rutting arrogance. He'd become somebody he didn't recognize. As she shivered in his arms, he knew that she was at his mercy and hated himself even more.

He relaxed his grip and let her slide down his body, then steadied her and stepped back. "I'm sorry." It wasn't enough, and he knew it. But what more could he say?

Molly couldn't reply. She stood paralyzed, trapped between her mind's incoherence and her body's swift response. It was as if her body had been slumbering for the last six years, until Chet Delaney had touched her. They stared at each other for an instant, and then he dropped his eyes.

He cleared his throat. "Molly, I don't know what—"

"Don't say anything else. It only makes it worse." She refused to look at him as she stepped carefully down off the curb and walked away with meticulously measured steps.

He watched her without moving until she reached the next corner, where she looked back once, then walked on at a quicker, surer pace.

Chapter 4

Molly awoke at seven-fifteen. She had returned to her room the night before in a weird state of mind, almost like suspended animation. The only way she had kept herself from crying and falling apart on the walk back to the motel had been by not thinking about what had happened with Chet.

Once she was safely back in her room, though, she hadn't been able to stop her mind from going over every single instant after he had stopped her from falling. Every sensation. Every look. Every word either of them had uttered. And the kiss. Oh Lord, the kiss . . .

Over and over she relived the kiss, as confusion, despair and guilt washed over her. Confusion because she could hardly believe it had really happened. Despair because she had been totally at Chet's mercy, unable to utter a single word to stop him. Guilt because the man who'd had such a devastating effect on her was a De-

laney who, her father had written, was up to something, and now her father was dead.

Lying wide-eyed in the dark, she thought about the
way Chet's chest had cradled her breasts and she
touched the lips his mouth had plundered with such
sweet ease. For one crazy moment she had wanted to
believe that her father had been drunk the day he died,
that in the preceding days he'd half emptied the bottle
of whiskey they'd found in the trailer and that the un-
accustomed alcohol had turned him suspicious and
paranoid.

"Idiot," she whispered savagely. "It would be in-
sane to trust Chet Delaney without knowing what Dad
meant in his last letter."

How, then, she wondered, was she to arm herself
against him? She had to find the strength within herself to go on with what she'd started.

Sleep finally had come, and it had been deep and
dreamless until she dragged herself from bed and
shuffled to the bathroom. The sluggishness flowed
from her body slowly with a warm shower. By the time
she was dressed and ready for breakfast, she had re-
gained a proper focus. She had a single, overriding
purpose for being in Sunset, and she could not allow
herself to explore any detours, titillating as they might
be.

Chet and the others might not have left for the well
site yet, but she wouldn't hide in her room until she was
sure he'd gone. She would rather face him now and get
it over with. She refused to admit that some traitorous
part of her longed to see his face.

From the doorway to the dining room, she spotted
Chet, Wilson and Boney Armbruister. Quickly scan-

ning the tables, she saw that the only unoccupied one was just beyond the table where the three men sat. She would have to walk past them to reach it.

Her first impulse was to turn and run, but she shook it off quickly. Squaring her shoulders, she walked to the buffet table to fill a plate and coffee cup. Then, after an instant's hesitation, she headed across the room to the only available table.

Her hope of reaching it before either of the three men noticed her was quickly dashed. Wilson grinned and called, "Good morning, Molly," when she was still only halfway to her destination. By the time she came even with his table, he was on his feet, pulling out the extra chair and saying, "Sit here."

Boney and Chet were looking up at her, but she kept her eyes on Wilson. "Thanks Wilson, but I'll sit over there."

His mouth dropped. "Aw, you're still mad at me."

"Nonsense. I was never mad at you," she said, laughing at his hangdog look.

He made a sweeping bow and held the chair. "Then prove it and sit down."

It seemed to Molly that Chet's gaze was burning her face. She still hadn't looked at him, and Wilson's insistence was making a spectacle of her. She felt incredibly self-conscious, and she couldn't keep ignoring the other two men without making a point of it.

All she wanted was for Wilson to sit down and stop calling attention to her. "Oh, all right." She set her plate and cup on the table and took the chair Wilson held. "Good morning, Boney... Chet."

Unable to put it off any longer, she lifted her eyes to meet Chet's. His keen inspection seemed to peel off the layers of her fragile composure, one at a time. One of his brows arched meaningfully.

"Morning, Molly." He reached for his coffee cup, a slight smile on his lips. "Did you sleep well?"

"Dropped off as soon as my head hit the pillow," she said brightly and busied herself adding pepper to her eggs. "How nice of you to ask." She set the shaker down and glanced at him. "And you?"

Hesitating for a moment, a faintly indecent twinkle in his eyes, Chet studied her lovely face. Her gray eyes were clear and overly bright until the sooty lashes swept down to hide them. Her skin had a dewy, fresh-scrubbed look, and as he watched, a tinge of pink spread over her cheeks. A light floral scent wafted to him, the smell of some feminine soap or cologne. Memories of holding her stirred an ache inside him. He took a swallow of coffee and set the cup down, reminding himself of several good reasons why he shouldn't feel the way she made him feel.

"Eventually." The word was as low and as intimate as a kiss.

Molly darted a quick, startled look at him. What had happened to the angry, aggressive man of last night? His smile poked fun at her, but his eyes held a more serious message. *Who do you think you're kidding, Molly Sinclair? You had as much trouble getting to sleep as I did.*

Wilson, bless him, was not one to tolerate another man claiming a woman's attention when he was around. He touched her wrist lightly. "Molly, change your mind and let me take you to the movie tonight."

She turned to him with relief. "Didn't you go last night?"

"Sure, but I'd like to see it again—with you."

"Thanks, Wilson, but I don't think so."

Boney muffled a laugh behind his napkin. Wilson kicked him under the table. "You keep turning me down, Molly, and you're going to ruin my reputation. Not to mention crushing my tender ego."

"Oh, I think your reputation is safe," Molly countered. "As for your ego, I'd say it's healthy enough to survive almost anything."

Wilson trailed a blunt finger down her cheek. "What do you have against me, sweetheart?"

"Maybe," Boney suggested, "fighting you off in the back of the Rialto Theater ain't her idea of a good time." Then he blushed, as though he'd surprised himself by speaking so boldly.

Molly threw both hands out, palms up, as though to say Boney had taken the words right out of her mouth. Boney laughed.

Wilson tried to look offended. "Good thing I don't give up easily. I enjoy a challenge, Molly."

Chet shoved his chair back and rose. Molly had been about to toss more teasing banter in Wilson's direction, but the sound made her lift her eyes, and she sobered immediately. He stood rubbing the back of his neck as he dragged himself from an absorbed study of her breasts. Not trying to disguise his approval of what he'd seen, he gave her a slow, insolent smile as he said, "I'll see you men out at the site."

Averting her eyes, Molly touched her napkin to her lips and pretended not to notice as she spooned strawberry jam onto her plate. Did Chet Delaney have any idea in the world how nervous he made her? She felt the impact of his gaze in the pit of her stomach.

"We're right behind you, boss," Boney said, getting up, too. He followed Chet to the kitchen, where Elsie would have their packed lunch buckets waiting.

"I hate to leave such good company, but..." Wilson moved to follow the others. But first he braced his hands on the table and leaned toward Molly. "I have an idea. Elsie always packs two sandwiches and enough dessert for a family of four. When you get your afternoon break, why don't you come out to the site and have lunch with me?"

Obviously the man was relentless in his pursuit of a woman. Odd that she didn't feel the least bit threatened by his persistence, when a mere look from Chet could shake her to her toes. "I won't be finished until two. You'll want lunch before that."

Wilson grinned, as though encouraged. Or perhaps he's simply oblivious to rejection, Molly thought, amused.

"For you, I'll wait."

"Don't. I wouldn't dream of eating part of your lunch, Wilson."

He straightened. "Forget lunch, then. Don't you want to see how we get the oil out of the ground?"

She couldn't tell him that she'd seen it plenty of times.

"Think about it." Throwing her a little salute, he headed for the kitchen.

The man is unflappable, Molly thought as she ate the last of her toast. She couldn't help liking Wilson, even if she couldn't imagine becoming romantically involved with him. He was certainly sure of himself, as Elsie had said, but his clear enjoyment of life, and of women, was almost refreshing. No dark depths there, Molly mused.

She couldn't help wondering if she wouldn't learn more about her father from Wilson simply by being friendly than she would ever learn from Chet. For one thing, Wilson didn't make her feel at such a disadvantage, as though she had to watch every word for telltale inflections.

Surely he wouldn't get the wrong idea if she simply drove out to the well site in the middle of the day and let him show her around, in the presence of his co-workers. It was an opportunity she couldn't pass up. She would take Lauren along for company.

Jude arched a disbelieving eyebrow when Molly asked if she could take Lauren with her to visit Wilson at the site. "I thought you weren't going to fall for his line."

"I haven't fallen for anything," Molly protested.

They were in the kitchen. Elsie was laying things out in preparation for cooking dinner, while Lauren sat at the kitchen table, absorbed in a coloring book.

"Ingrid will be jealous," Elsie observed.

"Good grief!" Molly sighed in exasperation. "There's nothing to be jealous about."

"If I were young and single," Elsie went on, ignoring Molly's aggrieved tone, "I'd set my cap for Chet Delaney."

The tip of Lauren's tongue poked out of the side of her mouth as she concentrated on coloring an umbrella purple. "They went off together last night," she announced. "I saw them."

Molly felt heat rush into her face as she blushed furiously. "We went for a walk. Look, I don't want anybody around here to get the idea that I'm interested in Chet Delaney. Or Wilson Formby, either. I'm not looking for a man, okay?''

"That's usually when you find one," Elsie chuckled. "When you're not looking."

"You people are impossible," Molly sputtered.

"Elsie's kidding you," Jude said. "Lauren, you don't have a swimming lesson today. You can go with Molly if you want to."

Lauren flashed her mother a grin and slapped her coloring book shut. "O-kaay! Let's go, Molly." As they passed the cashier's counter, Lauren informed Ingrid, "We're going to see Wilson."

Ingrid gave the child a startled look, then made a moue of displeasure. "On the job?"

"He offered to show us around," Molly explained.

Ingrid looked aggrieved. "Nothing to see but a bunch of sweaty men and some oil derricks."

"We won't be gone long," Molly said.

Outside, she chided Lauren, "Did you tell her where we were going just to upset her?"

Lauren turned up innocent green eyes. "She's already got a boyfriend. Marvin. They're going to get married. So she shouldn't be chasing Wilson, should she?"

"Well, I'm not sure she's chasing him." Lauren giggled and Molly tweaked her ponytail. "You're a mischief maker, young lady." She was beginning to wonder if it had been a good idea to invite Lauren, after all.

They had reached Molly's car. Broiler-temperature heat rushed out when she opened the door. Molly started the air conditioner, and they let the interior cool down for a few moments before they got in.

As they drove out of town, Lauren said, "You want me to tell Ingrid you really went to see Chet?"

"No, thank you! You've been helpful enough already. And I'm *not* going to see Chet."

Lauren gazed at her for a long moment. "Okay, but don't you like Chet, really?"

Molly sighed. "I like him fine. I like Wilson and David and the others fine, too."

Lauren gazed at her for another moment, then looked out at the road. They were approaching Sunset Lake. "Slow down after we cross the bridge," Lauren said. "I want to show you something."

The surface of the water was glass smooth. A few white sailboats drifted in the distance, and an elderly man and woman fished from the sandbar below the bridge. "They won't catch anything worth keeping," Lauren said with the scorn of a knowledgeable fisherman. "That's where all the out-of-towners fish." She pointed toward the north, Molly's side of the car. "See where the land sticks out over there?"

"Uh-huh. Looks like a little cove on the other side."

"That's where I caught my catfish."

"Then that's where we'll go Sunday."

"We better leave real early," Lauren advised. "So we can get a good place."

"You name the time."

As they reached the end of the bridge, Molly checked her rearview mirror. No car was in sight on the bridge or the straight stretch of highway beyond it. She braked to a near stop. "We've crossed the bridge. Now, what did you want to show me?"

Lauren was craning to see the bank that sloped steeply from the roadbed down to the lake. "That's where George drowned."

Two low metal rails edged the highway at that point. Her father's car would have crashed through the guardrails on its way down the incline, but these were undamaged. Obviously the rails had been replaced since the accident, and her father's car had left no visible marks on the rocky slope. The calm water of the lake glistened with the sun's reflected light. There was no hint that the placid setting had ever been the scene of a tragedy.

"I'm sorry he died," Molly murmured and pushed down on the accelerator, leaving the scene behind.

"Me, too. I bet it made his daughter real sad when she heard about it."

"I'm sure it did," Molly agreed.

Lauren sat forward in the seat. "Hey, you better slow down. We have to turn on that road up there."

When they reached the site, three men stood on a wooden platform near a drilling derrick, where a heavy cable was moving up and down in the well hole, driven by a noisy diesel engine. About a hundred yards west of the well sat two small travel trailers, with Delaney Drilling Company painted on their sides. One of the men on the platform jumped down and walked toward the car. It was Wilson Formby. Boney Armbruister waved a greeting from the platform. Molly didn't recognize the third man.

She rolled down her window. "We don't want to bother you if you're busy."

His grin was a slice of white in a grease-smeared face. A damp triangle of perspiration plastered the front of his work shirt to his chest. He poked his head in Molly's window. "I can take a break." He withdrew enough to open the car door, muttering from the corner of his mouth as she stepped out, "I see you brought a chaperone."

Lauren bounced out of her side of the car. "Hi, Wilson."

"Hi, kiddo."

Lauren wrinkled her nose. "It stinks out here."

Wilson laughed. "That's diesel fuel. You get used to it." He led them closer to the derrick and explained what Boney and the other man were doing, shouting to be heard over the noise of the engine. Then he yelled, "Let's go in the doghouse—the first trailer over there—so we can talk without hollering."

Molly glanced over at the second trailer as they followed Wilson up crude, wooden steps. Behind that trailer, a thick, black pole poked at the sky, supporting the temporary phone line installed at the site. Chet's car was parked beside the other trailer. She wondered if he'd seen them arrive.

The partitions inside the "doghouse" trailer had been removed, leaving a single room with a small galley-type kitchen on one end and a plastic couch and chairs on the other.

With the door closed, the noise outside was muffled. "This is where we cool off and eat lunch," Wilson said. He went to the sink to scrub his face and hands, using a bar of gritty, grease-cutting soap. Molly moved a tattered hunting magazine from a chair and sat down.

Wilson dried his hands and got three cans of cola from the small refrigerator. He popped the tabs and handed one to Molly and one to Lauren.

"Where's Chet?" Lauren asked.

"In the other trailer," Wilson told her.

"I think I'll go say hi."

Lauren was out the door before Molly could think of a way to stop her. In the silence that followed her exit, Wilson lowered himself to the edge of the chair facing Molly. "I didn't really think you'd come."

"I wanted to see a well being drilled," she said, as though she hadn't seen dozens with her father during her childhood. "Do you think you'll hit oil this time?"

He took a swallow of cola. "Who knows? Chet found traces of oil in the soil samples we took yesterday. That's encouraging."

"He told me the other geologist reported the same thing on samples taken from the first well, the one that turned out to be a dry hole."

He shrugged. "It happens all the time."

"Don't you think it's odd, the Delaneys taking Backus's advice to abandon that first hole?"

"No. That's what they paid him for."

"But he wasn't exactly reliable, was he? According to Chet, he drank on the job. You'd think, when they found out, they would have wanted to run some more tests."

He tilted his can and drained it. Then he set it on the linoleum-covered floor and leaned back in his chair, his elbows resting on its arms, his hands linked in front of him. "Nobody ever doubted Backus's reports. He was one of the best in the business."

Molly plucked at a split in the plastic covering on the arm of her chair. She asked casually, "In spite of the alcohol?"

He shrugged. "We didn't know he was drinking on the job until the day he died."

Molly looked up at him sharply. "You didn't? But Chet said he was staggering that day when he left work."

"He was. I was there. I tried to take his keys away from him, but he got in his car and locked the door. I had to jump out of his way to keep from being run down. But he was driving slow, probably couldn't see the road too well. I chased his car all the way out to the highway and ran along the shoulder, yelling for him to stop. He speeded up and left me behind."

"Yet you'd never seen him take a drink before that?"

"Not on the job."

She knew she was showing far too much interest in a supposed stranger, but Wilson seemed willing to answer her questions, and she had to take advantage of it. "Off the job?"

He hesitated, then said slowly, "I never actually saw him, but I suspected he was drinking in his room at the motel. I smelled it on his breath a couple of times."

Molly sank back in her chair, not wanting to hear what she was hearing. "Jude said he was a member of Alcoholics Anonymous, that he'd been sober for years."

"Yeah, but something set him off again."

"Do you have any idea what it could have been?"

"No, but the last couple of weeks before the accident, he seemed worried. He never said anything. It was just a feeling I got."

Molly stared at her hands. If her father had been worried enough to start drinking again, it had some connection to the Delaneys—something her father had discovered, or at least suspected, about them. She was convinced of it, because of what he had written in his last letter. Had he been trying to decide whether to confront them? Or turn them in?

"I was as surprised as anybody," Wilson was saying, "when George came out of that trailer, loop-legged and slurring his words. He must've been drinking in there all afternoon."

When Molly lifted her eyes, he was studying her quizzically. "Hey, you didn't know George Backus, did you?"

"Know him? Oh, no," she said quickly. Flicking her gaze away, she set her cola can down.

"Why all the questions, then?"

"Oh," she said lamely, "he was just on my mind. Chet was talking about him the other day, and on the drive out here, Lauren showed me where his car went off the road."

"I'm getting a funny feeling."

"About what?"

"Did you come out here to talk to me about Backus?"

She tried to sound surprised and amused. "Of course not. I wanted to get away from the motel for a while, that's all."

He laughed suddenly and slid out of his chair. Reaching for her hand, he pulled her to her feet.

"Why'd you bring Lauren? You aren't afraid to be alone with me, are you?"

The chair pressed against the backs of her legs. There was no room in the cramped space to step away from him. She tilted her head up and said lightly, "Should I be?"

He peered down at her, a quizzical lift at the corners of his mouth. She sensed he was thinking about kissing her. She couldn't let it happen. The only way to put some distance between them was to push him back with both hands and sidle away from the chair toward the door, where there was more room. It was awkward and embarrassing, but the alternative was worse. So she did it.

Surprised by her sudden move, he staggered backward, steadying himself by grabbing the arm of the chair. A line of white ringed his mouth, and a deep red crept up his neck. She'd humiliated him, and he was angry. She couldn't blame him. He must have interpreted her visit as a come-on. Oh, Lord, how awful.

She raked a nervous hand through her hair and gave him an apologetic smile. "This is all my fault, and I'm sorry. Let's be friends, Wilson."

He stared at her. "You want to be friends?" he muttered, as though laboriously deciphering words spoken in a foreign language.

"That's what I want, yes." Quickly, she stepped to the door and reached for the knob. "I'm afraid I gave you the wrong impression by coming here. Forgive me." She stepped out and closed the door behind her. Standing on the rickety wooden step, she took a deep breath to compose herself. She'd made a mess of things. What must Wilson be thinking of her?

As she stepped to the ground, the door of the second trailer opened, and Lauren and Chet came out. "It's time to go, Lauren," Molly said.

"Where's Wilson?" Lauren asked.

Aware of Chet's gaze on her, Molly said, "In the trailer."

"I gotta tell him goodbye," Lauren said, brushing past her.

In an unbelievably small voice, Molly said, "Hello, Chet." Behind her, the doghouse door banged shut as Lauren went inside.

"I'd appreciate it," Chet said stonily, "if you'd arrange your little flirtations somewhere else, when Wilson's off work."

It wasn't enough that she'd humiliated Wilson and made a fool of herself. She had to stand there and be insulted by Chet, too. His contemptuous tone went straight through her. "I'll try to remember that," she snapped, then turned on her heel and stalked away.

It occurred to her that stalking away from meetings with Chet was becoming a habit. She was thoroughly disgusted with herself by the time she reached her car.

Chapter 5

For the next two days, Molly sensed a definite coolness in both Wilson and Chet. Wilson didn't flirt or tease her anymore when she took his orders in the restaurant. And Chet seemed to be absorbed in something else whenever she was around. She might have believed he had other, more pressing things on his mind if she hadn't felt him studying her whenever her attention was engaged elsewhere. Even Ingrid was short with her. It made for an uncomfortable couple of days.

But the residents of the Hammond Motel lived too close to each other to maintain the silent—or, in Ingrid's case, not so silent—treatment for very long. Wilson was the first to break down. When Molly approached his table Friday evening, he gave her a smile and inquired, "How are you today, Molly? They're not working you too hard around here, are they?" He was the same, irrepressible Wilson again, behaving as though he'd never been out of sorts. She was forgiven.

Relieved, Molly responded in the same vein. Surprisingly, she'd missed talking to him. Now she admired his white shirt and tie. "You're looking mighty spiffy this evening."

"I'm taking Jill Rice to a dance at the armory."

Good, Molly thought. Maybe Ingrid would snipe at Jill now, instead of Molly. If only Chet would relent. He'd eaten an early dinner alone in the restaurant before Wilson arrived. Jude had waited on him, but Molly had passed his table several times. He'd had his head buried in a newspaper and appeared not to notice her.

After her evening stint in the restaurant, Molly started to her room. She'd bought a paperback suspense novel at the drugstore that morning, but she felt too restless to read. Nor was she interested in going for a walk after her shower; she'd been on her feet long enough for one day.

"Molly?"

With a gasp of surprise, she stumbled back against the wall. When she saw Chet approach out of the shadows where the hall angled toward Jude's apartment, she released a long breath and took the few remaining steps to her door. "I didn't see you," she said, feeling foolish.

"Didn't mean to startle you." He came toward her.

"My mind was wandering, I guess," she said.

"You look tired."

"We didn't have time to sit down for a minute this evening." She cleared her throat and pulled her door key from a shirt pocket. But she found it impossible to

open the door while he was there. Had he been waiting for her? He wore shorts and athletic shoes.
"You've been out walking."

"Yes." He debated telling her that he'd been back
from his walk for half an hour and had waited in the
hall to speak to her. But he decided to leave it to her to
guess whether it was a chance meeting or planned.
"I've been wanting to apologize for what I said to you
the other day at the site."

"Oh." She turned the key over and over in her hand.
"That's all right. I shouldn't have interrupted the
men's work. I wasn't thinking."

"It was no big deal. I shouldn't have gotten ticked
off."

"I acted pretty childish myself."

His gaze skimmed down her, lingering on her lips.
"We seem to bring out the worst in each other. It's
damned disconcerting."

"I don't know what you mean."

"Yes, you do." He gazed at the pulse beating in the
hollow of her throat, then lifted his eyes to hers.

There was no point in continuing to deny what was
so patently true. "I think we got off on the wrong
foot." She smiled hesitantly. "Maybe we should start
over."

"That's what I had in mind." He lounged against the
wall as she gazed at him. "Would you like to take in a
movie tomorrow night?"

"I—I can't ask Jude to get off early. Saturday's our
busiest night, and there's no one else to help her."

"We could go to the late show at ten-thirty."

She felt a sharp twinge, remembering what had happened on their last outing together. She didn't know if it was fear or excitement. "Well..."

He reached out, gently cupping her chin in his hand so that she had no choice but to look directly at him. "You said we should start over. Did you mean it?"

At the end of his words, she found herself staring at his mouth. She wanted him to kiss her, she realized, and that frightened her. She was shocked to know that fear could be a source of exhilaration. She nodded. "All right. I'd like to go to the movie with you."

The tension that had been in him all evening eased a little. He hadn't known until that moment how worried he'd been that she would say no. His head swam with strange sensations. Over the past two days, the voice in his mind that had warned him to stay away from her had weakened. He was thirty-two years old, yet there had been no other time, no other place, no other woman, that had made him ache like this. And he knew so little about her. Maybe, he told himself, the mystery of her was part of the magic, and when he knew her better it would go away.

She watched the flitting emotions play across his face. It gave her time to gain some measure of composure, to realize that she'd actually been considering inviting him in. She knew that would be a mistake. She took a long, cleansing breath and found she could meet his gaze squarely. She gripped the key tightly in her hand, the only outward sign that she was fighting herself. "Good night, Chet."

He had his own battles to fight. He accepted her dismissal as a sort of reprieve. "Good night."

When he left her alone, Molly missed the lock twice before she managed to insert the key. Only then did she become aware that her hands were trembling. She stepped into the dark bedroom and closed the door behind her.

After engaging the bolt and turning on the light, she gazed at the key in her hand. Once she had willed steadiness into her fingers, the key had opened her door easily. If only it were as simple to unlock the secrets hidden in Chet Delaney's mind.

The wardrobe Molly had brought to Sunset contained nothing very dressy. After work and a quick shower Saturday night, it took only a moment to select a full, blue-and-white striped cotton skirt and a gauzy white blouse. She slid her bare feet into white sandals and was ready when Chet tapped on her door a few minutes later.

"Hi," she greeted him.

As he looked down at her, he thought that she was like a lovely, fragile china doll—until you looked deeply into her eyes and found the strength and fire.

"Hi," he said steadily.

She stepped into the hall and pulled her door shut.

He took a bracing breath and gripped her arm. "Let's get out of here. Lauren found out we're going to a movie and wants to go with us."

"I wouldn't mind—" she started to say as he propelled her toward the lobby doors.

"I would. I told her it would be after midnight when we got back, and she's too young to be up that late." He pushed open a glass door and ushered her through.

She smiled and impulsively reached for his hand. She instantly regretted the intimacy of the gesture, but it was too late to change her mind. "I'll bet she loved hearing that."

Chet had half expected her to insist on taking Lauren to act as a buffer between them. Now he felt something unknot in his stomach. He grinned and curled his fingers around hers. "She informed me that she'd stayed up past midnight hundreds of times." He opened the passenger door of his car, and she scooted in. He went around the hood and got in. "When I last saw her, she was headed to the apartment to ask her mother if she could come with us."

"She'll be mad at both of us."

"Yeah." She had a striking face, feminine angles and soft skin, all of it dominated by those expressive, velvet-gray eyes. A man could drown in those eyes. He imagined them sparkling with joy, and soft and languorous with love. Then glazed with passion. He could think of dozens of ways he'd like to make love to her. In consternation, he dragged his mind away from a particularly erotic fantasy. He usually had more control over his thoughts. He started the car and drove out of the parking lot. "She'll get over it."

As he directed his attention to the street, Molly felt the atmosphere in the car shift. For a moment she'd been convinced that she should never have agreed to go out with him. The way he looked at her sometimes scared her. It was contemplative and not altogether friendly. She was certain he didn't completely trust her. Exactly why or in what way he found her suspect, she didn't know. But somehow she had to get past her own fear and Chet's distrust if she was to discover the truth about her father's death.

She rested her head against the seat and gazed out the side window at the dark glass fronts of the local businesses. Main Street was deserted. Like a ghost town, she mused, and realized the thought had come from her own mood. Sometimes, with Chet, she felt disconsolate. Other times, galvanized by energy, she felt like a tightrope walker, crossing a treacherously deep chasm without a net. She shook off the thought, determined to enjoy the movie and relax with him.

Carrying popcorn and colas, they found their way along the darkened aisle. The movie credits were already rolling as they found seats in the middle of the theater.

Molly settled back, glad that there was no need for the moment to make conversation. She munched her popcorn and soon became engrossed in the film . . . so engrossed, in fact, that she almost forgot where she was and with whom. Until Chet draped his arm around the back of her chair and his fingers began toying with the curls behind her ear.

She only had to shift away to communicate her displeasure. But she didn't. Her mind told her to set the ground rules for their relationship right then and there. She'd had no trouble spelling it out for Wilson. Friendship. That was all she wanted from him, and it was all she could want from Chet. But still she didn't move.

Chet ran his thumb down the side of her neck, and a shiver of excitement skipped through her. When he nudged her head toward his shoulder, she didn't resist, which made her whispered words sound ridiculously hollow.

"I don't think this is a good idea."

"I'm not sure I do, either," he murmured, then turned his face into her sweetly scented curls. Shifting, he brushed his lips against her forehead, tasting her skin with the tip of his tongue. "You make me think dangerous thoughts."

Molly shivered. "Stop," she whispered. She was all heat and softness inside. She had the feeling that if he didn't stop now, she would let him do anything. Already she'd lost track of the movie. She was in danger of forgetting that they were in a public theater.

"I think I'd better." The whispered words were raspy. He lifted his head and stared at the movie screen, but his jaw rested against her forehead, and his arm was warm around her shoulders, his hand languidly stroking her arm.

Molly stifled a moan of despair and fixed her eyes on the screen. She had no idea what those celluloid people were doing. Their dialogue now seemed senseless. Make-believe people in a make-believe crisis.

What would happen when she and Chet got back to the motel? She wouldn't think about that now. Molly closed her eyes and willed calmness into her system. If she were to get close to Chet, close enough for him to talk freely about her father, she had to learn to hold her own with him.

If she hadn't still been grieving for her father, missing him, her emotions confused and close to the surface, Chet would never have gotten to her. Ever since her marriage had ended, she'd managed to keep the upper hand in her relationships with men. Chet Delaney would have been no different, she told herself, if he hadn't entered her life when she was so vulnerable.

The movie ended. Finally. Molly forced herself to talk about the actors and the story line on the drive back to the motel. Chet tossed in a few observations of his own, but she had the distinct feeling that he was humoring her.

She didn't reach for his hand this time as they walked from his car toward the door that opened directly into the hallway. The atmosphere between them now was too electric for her to risk touching him. She kept a step ahead, wanting only to reach her room and shut herself in so she could feel safe. They had reached the door when Chet spoke.

"Molly," he murmured, and the warmth of his breath ruffled a wisp of hair over her ear. "Don't run away from me."

She swiveled, realizing too late that it was a dreadful mistake. He was so close that his body brushed her breasts, making her nipples ache with longing. Molly clasped her hands between them as though, by some miracle, that would make her impregnable to him. She tried to lean back and felt the solid, unyielding door behind her.

"Don't be silly. I wasn't running."

He smiled faintly. "Metaphorically speaking." He examined her upturned face, his eyes moving lazily over her features with the physical impact of a lover's touch. Yet his look went beyond the surface, delving deeper than any man had ever done before. He wanted to see into her mind. It alarmed her. At the same time, she knew that if he weren't a Delaney, she wouldn't even want to resist.

"You were running in your mind," he murmured knowingly.

It was silly, but she pretended ignorance. "I don't know what you're talking about. What was I running from?"

"I'll have to show you." She had such soft, flawless skin, he mused as he ran a fingertip over her cheekbone. "We set off sparks in each other. You're afraid of starting a fire we can't put out." He gently traced the line of her earlobe, idly fingering the gold stud she wore.

She could barely breathe. "Aren't you?" she whispered.

"I'm aware of the danger." Slowly, his eyes skimmed over her face again. Yes, between them they would create a roaring, spreading conflagration, and they would have no control over where it would end. Wildfire.

He knew all that, yet when he was near her, a reckless excitement overcame logic. He wanted to make love to her out of doors with fragrant grass for their bed and the star-studded sky for a canopy. He wanted to see her naked body bathed in moonlight. He wanted to watch the changes in her features—the softening, the yielding.

Along with the recklessness, he recognized a sense of inevitability. He was going to do those things, he thought as something knotted in his stomach. The only question was when. It was an acceptance and a vow.

"The danger draws me. It draws both of us, Molly."

He pressed closer, his unsteady breath feathering her lips. He understood her much too well.

"I'd like to take you to some romantic spot for dinner. There would be candlelight and wine." His low voice had a lulling effect on her. "Afterward, I'd drive into the country and make love to you beneath the stars."

His words painted a vivid picture that she found almost irresistible. It was like the feeling she'd had as a teenager when her father had taken her to see the Grand Canyon. She had stood there paralyzed by fear, seeing herself plummeting down. She had seen it so clearly that it was almost as if something inside her urged her to step into the void.

Chet affected her the same way. He would be a fiercely demanding lover, the kind women longed for, even knowing they might be destroyed by the experience. Heaven help her, she wanted him, more than she had known she could ever want a man. She ached for him, knowing he could very well be the enemy. It was that knowledge that made her want to run.

"No." But the denial was so weak it was barely audible, when she had intended it to be clear and strong. "We could never be casual lovers. I—I can't take the risk."

"You've already started," he corrected, then pulled her into his arms and kissed her with a need his quiet words had hidden.

It was like being struck by lightning. She was falling, falling, going wherever he would take her. She had no will of her own. His seeking mouth shot heat through her. It mingled with the panicked excitement that had her clinging while her saner self told her to pull away. Her response was stunning, boiling up from inside her like a raging torrent crashing through its confining banks. With both hands, he clasped her head, tilting it back so that he could have his fill of her.

Chet was on fire with need that had him fantasizing about tearing away the cotton and silk of her clothing—everything that separated her skin from his hands. He did battle with the urge by focusing on her mouth, exploring, probing, savoring, possessing.

He could no longer lie to himself. He had wanted her in his arms like this since the day he first laid eyes on her, even though she was not the frivolous, inconstant, safe kind of woman he ordinarily let get close to him, the kind with whom he could take and give pleasure, and then move on. Molly would lodge in his mind, and he might never forget her. What perverse instinct was it that made him want her with a force that bordered on madness? It wasn't his way, yet he pulled her closer and plundered.

Molly's body yielded to his as though it had no form of its own. Her mouth seemed fused to his, while a part of her mind issued feeble commands to break free. The other part was compelling her to submit to his demands—and make demands of her own. Something wild and frenzied had taken up residence within her. It was feeding her reckless, dangerous thoughts, that, if acted on, threatened to loose something in her that was at once untamed and untamable.

The wildness that her body had harbored unknowingly until now wanted out. And, oh, it was tempting to free it, to cut the reins and let it rampage where it would. Let it carry her to the primitive regions where she had never ventured before.

From whence she might not find her way back. For an instant, fear overcame the compulsion to let go. She tore at the hands that held her head immobile and wrenched her mouth from his. "No!" The word was spoken on a rising note of panic. "I want you to let me go."

Chet's fevered mind struggled to make sense of her words. Frustration at having his clamoring desire thwarted paralyzed him for a moment, but then reason managed to reassert itself. He wasn't used to having his emotions battered so tumultuously, and he scrambled to find his balance.

"I've never forced a woman in my life," he said, amazed at the calmness in his tone, "and I don't intend to start now. I can wait for you to come to me."

His arrogant confidence gave her the spurt of angry energy she needed. "Don't hold your breath," she snapped, then twisted sideways to fumble for the doorknob. Her hand shook so badly she was unable to get a grip on the knob immediately.

All at once she was swamped by despair. "I don't see why—" she cried, her voice splintering like breaking glass "—why we can't enjoy each other's company without this—this—"

"Passion?"

She couldn't look at him. "Insanity," she amended.

"Yes," he mused in agreement. "That's it, isn't it? Well, we'll do it any way you want, Molly."

She could have dealt with it more easily if he'd argued, but his calm, reasoned acquiescence gave rise to more confusion. It was as if he was willing to accept defeat in one skirmish because he was sure of winning the ultimate victory.

At last her unsteady hand managed to get a firm grip on the doorknob. She twisted it and jerked the door open.

Chet said nothing as she plunged into the motel hallway, made no move to catch the heavy door as it slammed shut again with such force that its steel frame vibrated and the shattering noise echoed and dissolved in the after-midnight silence. Then, from far away, he heard the hoot of an owl. A lonely sound. Mocking, almost.

He leaned against the motel, one knee bent to brace himself with the sole of his shoe against the brick wall. He needed a moment to sort through what had happened.

He hadn't meant to kiss her like that. At least, he had promised himself he wouldn't. If he kissed her at all, he'd told himself, it would be a friendly, brotherly kiss, over as quickly as it began. He liked women; he knew them. He'd always been able to sense how far to go, what liberties he could take without sending the wrong message or losing control of the situation. Women had challenged him before, and he had never felt threatened by that. It was part of the male-female game, he'd always thought. He knew the game well, played by the rules. As long as everybody played by the rules, nobody got hurt.

With a word, a look, Molly could make him forget the rules, forget even that it was a game.

Something different, something unique, was happening between himself and Molly. He couldn't quite identify what it was. If he knew what was good for him, he mused, he would take her at her word. A relationship without passion. That was what she claimed she wanted. They were to enjoy each other's company and let it end there. They were to be friends.

Usually he *did* know what was good for him, Chet reflected, but with Molly he was ready to throw caution to the wind. He took deep, steadying breaths of the warm night air and waited for the need that was still a dull ache in his groin to ease.

But the sense of inevitability that had settled on him when he held her in his arms remained. He wanted her, and he would have her. It was written in their stars.

Chapter 6

When Molly went to the Hammonds' suite Sunday morning, Lauren was dressed and waiting for her with two cane fishing poles. Cramming a wide-brimmed straw hat on her head, she handed a similar hat to Molly and said, "You ran off without me last night."

Molly made a helpless gesture. "I apologize. But it was awfully late."

"You and Chet just didn't want me tagging along."

Lauren was too smart to bamboozle, so Molly merely shrugged. "What can I say?"

Lauren eyed her, clearly trying to decide whether to forgive her or not. Then she tugged at the brim of her hat. "We have to stop at the bait shop on the way." Nothing, it seemed, would be allowed to interfere with their fishing trip.

Before they left the motel, Molly found Jude in the restaurant kitchen. "We're leaving for the lake now," she said. "I don't know when we'll be back."

Jude, who was mixing dough for biscuits, waved a distracted goodbye. "I know Lauren's safe with you."

Lauren tugged at Molly's hand. "Let's *go*."

They drove to the bait shop, which was next door to a convenience store. "Let's get some food to take with us," Lauren suggested. "We can have a jungle lunch."

Her words sent a sharp stab of memory through Molly. "Jungle lunch? Where did you hear that expression?"

"That's what George called it."

Molly had known the expression all her life. Whenever she'd gone fishing with her father, they'd always picked up a "jungle lunch"—a sackful of junk food— to take along. When she'd been a child, fishing trips were the only times she was allowed to munch fat, salt and sugar-laden food to her heart's content.

Lauren, it seemed, expected to spend most of the day at the lake. "We should have brought a sack lunch from the restaurant," Molly said, suppressing a smile.

"It's too late now," Lauren said happily. Clearly, she looked forward to the rare occasions when she could pig out on empty calories as much as Molly had as a child.

"You're right. Let's see what we can find."

A half hour later, they arrived at the lake supplied with earthworms for the fish, and cookies, candy, chips and frankfurters for themselves. Directed by Lauren, Molly drove off the highway, taking a graveled lane that roughly followed the lake's shoreline. They left the car where the lane ended. Carrying poles, bait and food, they walked the last three hundred yards to a small cove. No other fishermen were in sight.

"Hey, looks like we have it all to ourselves," Molly observed.

"That's why I wanted to get here early," Lauren said. "So we could choose the best place to sit."

The shade provided by several trees was at least fifty yards from the water's edge. Molly donned the straw hat Lauren had given her, and they settled on the bank to bait their hooks.

Molly tossed her line in and tipped her hat forward to shade her face. Beside her, Lauren said, "I hope I catch another big catfish today."

Molly leaned forward, arms resting on her bent knees, her pole held loosely in both hands. "Like the one you caught when you came here with George?"

"Yeah."

"You liked George a lot, didn't you?"

Lauren nodded, staring at the red-and-white plastic cork attached to her line that floated in the water. "I didn't even know about the accident, 'cause I was at my friend Cassie's house when it happened. I slept over. When I went to George's room the next day, he wasn't there. It was Sunday. We were supposed to go fishing."

"Nobody told you what happened to him?"

"No. Mom didn't see me when I came home. She was in the restaurant. I left my overnight case in my room and went straight to George's room. Mr. Delaney, Chet's uncle, came to the door."

"Mr. Delaney spent the night in George's room?"

Lauren nodded. "Chet, too. I guess there wasn't anyplace else for them to stay."

"Where had they been staying before?"

"Another motel. They came to town a few days before, but I hadn't met them 'til that morning. When they told Mom about George's accident, they said they gave up their room at the other motel 'cause they planned to go back to Houston that day, so Mom said they could use George's room. Mr. Delaney left the next day, but Chet stayed to work in George's place."

Molly was trying to assimilate what Lauren was telling her, trying to fit it into a logical sequence of events. "So it was Chet and his uncle who came to tell your mother about the accident?"

"Yeah. They were out there at the well that day."

"When George left work?"

"I think so."

Molly remembered Chet's saying that he and his uncle had been in Sunset for a few days when the accident occurred. Why hadn't he mentioned that they'd been at the site when her father drove away, headed back to town? And if her father had been so obviously drunk, as everyone kept telling her, why hadn't somebody stopped him? She kept coming back to that question. Wilson seemed to have been the only one who even tried. Yet Chet and his uncle and at least one other employee, the roughneck, had been there, too.

She would have to ask Chet about it, she realized. It wouldn't be easy to elicit information if he didn't want to give it, nor to explain why she was so interested in the death of a man she wasn't even supposed to have known. Nothing was easy with Chet. He confused her, and she didn't want to be confused, especially now, when she needed all her wits about her to dig out the truth about her father's death.

But she couldn't do the sensible thing and stay away from him, either. Not that staying away from him would keep him from her thoughts. Not after last night. He was there, even when he wasn't *there*.

She'd lain awake for what seemed like hours after she'd left him last night, unable to get him out of her head and her senses. Long after she'd removed herself from his physical presence, she could still see him, hear him, smell his scent, taste him.

Even now, just thinking about it, she felt the weakness creeping into her. Perhaps she and Lauren could stay at the lake all day. There was enough snack food in their sack to provide their dinner as well as their lunch. When they returned to the motel, she could stay in her room until morning. Coward, she accused herself. She let out a long, weary breath and reached for the paper sack.

It was almost ten on Monday morning when Molly left her room and went to the restaurant for breakfast. She hadn't seen Chet at all the previous day, having kept to her room after returning from the lake, cowardice or no. She didn't know if he'd hung around the motel all day or gone out, and she told herself she didn't care. What had happened Saturday night was a simple failure of good sense, she kept insisting to herself. The reckless thing inside her was again contained, and she was in control. It was now a matter of being careful when Chet was around. *Very* careful.

When Molly carried her dirty breakfast dishes to the kitchen, Jude was remarking to Elsie that Chet hadn't been himself that morning. Molly found that she was intensely curious for more details. Had Saturday night been responsible for Chet's mood?

"Who was he, then?" she inquired.

Jude smiled and indicated a black lunch bucket sitting on the counter. "He forgot his lunch. Didn't say boo to anyone at breakfast, then bolted out of here before I could catch him and give him that."

Elsie snorted. "He ate enough breakfast to hold him 'til tomorrow morning."

"He always eats a big breakfast," Jude said. "All the men do. But they want their lunch buckets full, just the same."

"I'd put that in the refrigerator and give it to him tomorrow morning. I expect he'll drive back to town if he gets hungry before evening."

Molly agreed with Elsie. Chet was a big boy, more than capable of taking care of himself.

She forgot their brief conversation until Jude brought it up again as Molly was about to begin her afternoon break. She thrust her head into the kitchen one last time to make sure she wasn't needed again before going to her room. Elsie was rummaging in the pantry, and Jude was relaxing at the table with a glass of iced tea.

"Do you know if the mail's come?" Jude asked.

"It hasn't," Molly told her. She'd just checked the box in the lobby and found the outgoing mail still in it. There had been several envelopes addressed by Jude to businesses she dealt with, and another that she'd puzzled over briefly. It was addressed to somebody in Maine, and the return address was "Petroleum Investors, Inc.," with a Fort Worth post office box number. She thought the Formby brothers lived in Fort

Worth and decided they must have a small oil-related venture going on the side. "Is there anything else I can do before I leave?"

"We have everything under control here," Jude said. "What are you planning to do now?"

"I don't know. Read, maybe. Why?"

"Oh, I thought if you didn't have anything better to do, you might take Chet's lunch out to the site. He must be hungry enough to eat a bear by now. I'd do it, but I promised to take Lauren to town for new shoes."

Molly started to say she'd take Lauren shopping instead, but changed her mind before the thought became words. She was frightened of seeing Chet because of what he made her feel, yet she sensed he held the key to her discovering what had really happened to her father. If she delivered Chet's lunch, perhaps she could talk to him about her father while he ate. If she showed an interest in his work, it shouldn't be too difficult to bring the former geologist into the conversation.

When she arrived at the site, Wilson's and Chet's cars were parked between the two trailers, but she saw no one. Wilson and Boney were probably taking a break in the doghouse. Chet might be with them, or he could be working in the other trailer. The noise of the two air conditioners, added to the sound of the drilling pump and the hum of a brisk, hot wind, would have covered the sounds of stampeding cattle.

She chose the second trailer and knocked. "Coming!" Chet called. A moment later, the door opened.

Molly held up the lunch bucket. "Jude was afraid you'd starve before dinnertime."

After a long, speculative stare through his reading glasses, he took the lunch bucket from her hand. "I was beginning to feel a bit hollow. Thanks for going to the trouble.''

Molly caught a strand of her hair as the wind whipped it across her cheek. ''No trouble.''

It seemed much longer than a day since he'd seen her. She was even lovelier than he remembered, he thought, with her hair whipping around her face. The steady gusts flushed her cheeks and made her black curls dance. ''Are you in a hurry to get back to town?''

''Not really.'' She peered beyond him to the interior of the trailer. Did she actually want to be alone with him in there? She shook off her sudden doubt. ''I was kind of hoping you'd offer me something to drink.''

''Would you like something to drink?'' he murmured, giving her an easy, lopsided grin.

''I thought you'd never ask.'' She brushed past him, looking around her curiously. Like the doghouse, this trailer had been stripped of partitions. The small kitchen was at one end, a sofa and chair at the other, with work counters and shelves built along both walls in between. The wind buffeting the trailer made it creak and groan as though in pain.

He removed his glasses and laid them on the counter beside the telephone, watching her quick inspection of the trailer as she set down the lunch bucket. ''There's root beer and cola, and I just made a fresh pot of coffee.''

She settled on a stool near the counter, glancing at the automatic drip coffeemaker. ''Mmm...coffee, I think.''

He took a foam cup from beneath the counter, filled it and set it in front of her. Then he got a root beer from the refrigerator, pulled another stool up next to hers, opened his lunch bucket and unwrapped a meatloaf sandwich.

He was so close to her that her arm inadvertently brushed his. Nervously, she leaned away and took a swallow of coffee. "This is delicious," she said.

"I've spent a lot of time perfecting my coffee making. You drink gallons when you're sitting a well. I tried four different brands of coffee makers before I settled on that one. The coffee's a special blend. I get it from a gourmet shop in Houston."

She took another sip. "I'm impressed."

"Don't be." He unwrapped a dill pickle and took a crunchy bite. "Coffee's about the only thing I can make." He turned sideways on the stool, facing her. "Are you a good cook?"

"Only average."

He reached out and wrapped a tousled curl around his finger. "Average is good enough. You're better than average at other things." She turned her head, pulling her hair from his grasp. He gave her a teasing smile.

"What things?" she asked, and knew immediately that it was the wrong question. She glanced away from him in confusion.

"Kissing, to begin with."

She knew better than to ask what he had in mind to end with. "Swell," she muttered on a frustrated breath.

"I mean it." He cupped her chin in his hand and made her look at him. "Everybody's kisses are different, unique."

"You've researched the subject?"

"You could say that." With his thumb he traced the outline of her bottom lip. There was a sweetness there, and a rich sensuality. "Do you think it has something to do with the shape of the mouth?"

"I wouldn't know," she managed to say as his thumb swept slowly back and forth beneath her bottom lip. "Aren't you going to finish your lunch?"

"Sure." Chet dropped his hand and reached for his half-eaten sandwich. "There's another sandwich here." She shook her head. He unwrapped another foil package. "A chocolate-chip cookie?"

She took one and, nibbling at it, swept her gaze down the counter where they sat. Reaching out, she tapped a stack of small, fanfold paper sheets with one finger. "What's this?"

"Seismograph logs."

The jagged marks on the paper were similar to the lines on an electrocardiogram. Molly had seen such logs before; her father had brought them home a number of times. "Where do you get them?"

"From a seismograph—an instrument that amplifies and records small movements in the earth. We drill a hole in the ground and set off explosives. Shock waves from the explosion bounce off underground rocks, and the seismograph measures them."

"These peaks on the log are measurements?"

He nodded and reached around her, his chest pressing against her back. "See this? The deeper the peak, the longer it takes the shock waves to reach the underground formation. The time it takes them to reach a rock layer and return to the surface tells us how deep the layer lies. It also gives us clues to the type of rock formation."

She bent to study the diagram he held. "Does it tell you if there's oil?"

"No, it's not that exact a science."

She nodded. "If it were, I suppose you'd hit oil every time."

"Right. Oil collects in underground traps. Seismograph logs help us locate sites where the rock formations are likely to contain oil. You collect all the scientific information you can, and it's still a gamble, with the odds stacked against you."

"Are these the logs for the well you're drilling now?"

"Yes." He reached his other hand around her and flipped over another page, imprisoning her between his arms. His head was so close to hers that his cheek brushed her hair. She could hear him breathing. "See this section here? The formation is quite favorable for finding oil. Very nearly ideal."

"I'll keep my fingers crossed for good luck," she murmured. His breath was warm on her ear. It made her want to shiver and hug herself.

"You do that. God knows we can use all the luck we can get." She raised her coffee cup to her mouth as he nuzzled his face into her hair. "Mmm, you smell good. What's that perfume?"

Molly barely avoided choking on the coffee. "I'm not wearing perfume," she managed as his breath heated her neck. Gripping her cup, she slid forward off the stool and poured herself more coffee, which she took to the sofa at the other end of the trailer.

Smiling at her nervousness, Chet refilled his cup and joined her on the sofa. Settling back, he made himself comfortable. "I feel much better now. It was sweet of you to think of my lunch."

"I didn't. Jude asked me to bring it."

"Ah. I must remember to thank her."

She turned her head to give him a sharp scrutiny. "You 'forgot' your lunch on purpose, didn't you?"

He gave her an injured look. "How could I have known someone would bring it out here, much less that it would be you?" He leaned over to tug on a curl. "Not that I'm not delighted to see you."

She shifted to set her cup on the floor near her feet. She rested her elbow on the arm of the sofa and her chin in her cupped palm. "You knew Jude would be too busy to traipse out here herself. Who else was there but me?" She sent him an accusing glance from beneath half-lowered lashes. "It was a calculated risk. Or at least a Freudian slip."

"Fate," he countered as he ran a hand lightly down her back. "Wonderful, isn't it?"

"Fate, my eye."

Not bothering to conceal a grin, Chet took a few moments to finish his coffee and dispose of the cup. Molly had retrieved her cup and was taking slow, savoring sips.

"Is Lauren still mad at us for running out on her Saturday night?"

She'd expected him to continue needling her, and the abrupt switch surprised her. He was confusing her again. She frowned into her coffee. "She wanted to go fishing, so she decided to forgive us."

"Catch anything?"

"Nothing big enough to keep. It was pleasant getting away for the day, anyway."

"Lauren's a great kid."

"Uh-huh." She set her cup down again and turned to look at him. "She talked about George Backus. His death hit her hard."

"I gather he was a sort of surrogate grandfather to her."

He was watching her calmly, and she looked away for a moment. Her brow knitted as she brought her eyes back to his. "Lauren said you were out here when Backus left the site the day of the accident."

"That's true," he said easily, watching her continue to frown in consideration. "I was."

"You didn't tell me that," she said, then rose. Stuffing her hands into her jeans pockets, she stared out the window. Wilson and Boney were moving about the well platform now, their eyes slitted against the wind that tossed dust into their faces.

"It didn't seem pertinent."

"Pertinent?" With a sudden exasperation that surprised them both, Molly whirled around. "You saw him leave the trailer, staggering. You saw him get into his car." She gestured, then dropped her hand. "Why didn't you stop him?"

Intrigued by her abrupt intensity, he watched her. "Correction. I didn't see him when he left. We were all in the doghouse, except for Wilson, who did try to stop him." He rose and walked toward her, eyeing her thoughtfully. "Just as a matter of idle curiosity, why are you so interested in Backus?"

"It's—it's weird, that's all." Knowing the words hadn't come out the way she wanted them to, Molly pushed a hand through her hair. "Lauren's talked about him so much that I almost feel as though I knew him." She forced herself to meet his probing gaze.

"She spent a lot of time with him, and she's sure he wasn't drinking."

"Molly..." He lifted his hands to her shoulders, massaging gently. "Lauren is a naive, trusting eight-year-old."

She felt heat spreading slowly from her shoulders throughout her body and ordered herself to concentrate. "Jude doesn't believe it, either." She let out a long, weary breath. "It's all very mysterious, Chet. George Backus came here from Dallas in February, and everybody says he seemed perfectly content. He refused to go to the bars with the other men. David Formby called him a boring teetotaler. Lauren heard them arguing one night."

He stifled the need to gather her into his arms until she'd forgotten this Backus tangent she was on, forgotten everything but him. With an effort, he kept his hands still. He suspected his motives were mixed. He knew he wanted her; he'd never had such difficulty keeping his hands off a woman before. At times, he thought ruefully, he managed to convince himself that it was meant to be and to resist was futile. It was less troubling when he could shift the responsibility to fate and off himself.

He also admitted that Molly's questions about Backus made him feel slightly guilty. It was true that he hadn't seen the man leave the site that day, but he'd spent quite a bit of time with him on the two preceding days. He couldn't help wondering if there had been signs that Backus was troubled about something, that he'd returned to the bottle—signs that Chet might have picked up on if he'd paid more attention.

"How did you know Backus was from Dallas?" he asked, searching her face. "Have you been investigating the accident?"

"No," she insisted quickly. "Somebody told me he lived there. It must have been Jude." She dropped her eyes.

"You called it a mystery, and you've apparently talked to several people about it. That sounds like an investigation to me."

Gracelessly, she stepped back out of his grasp and forced a lightness into her voice. "You think I'm so bored I've resorted to playing detective?"

"Maybe," he mused, then grinned wolfishly. "If you're bored, I can think of much better ways to inject some excitement into your life."

"I'm sure." She shook off the lingering fear that he was on to her masquerade. "But we'll have to explore that later, when there's more time. Right now, I have to get back to town."

"I'll hold you to it," he murmured.

"By explore, I meant talk," she told him as she felt little tingles of excitement begin. She fought them down and moved to the door. "Later, Chet."

"Count on it," he said confidently as she opened the door and stepped into the blazing sun. The wind wasn't as strong as it had been when she'd entered the trailer. Thank goodness, Molly thought. She had been afraid the wind was going to be the precursor to one of west Texas's legendary dust storms, but the worry seemed to have been unwarranted, for now. She waved at Wilson and Boney as she got into her car.

* * *

With the passing of the wind, the heat came back, as fierce and as unrelenting as ever. Molly heard several restaurant patrons that evening talking about the area farmers' desperate need for rain. Chet, Wilson and Boney had eaten hurriedly and retreated to their rooms. Molly saw Chet leave the motel in shorts and a tank top a few minutes later.

None of the diners lingered long that evening, in fact, because the restaurant's air-conditioning compressor had broken down that afternoon, and a serviceman was still working on it. Jude had positioned big fans in the four corners of the restaurant, but all they accomplished was to keep the warm air moving.

Business was light, and Molly had frequent opportunities to sit down and sip ice water. During a lull, when the restaurant was without a single diner, Ingrid, who was no longer snubbing Molly, called to her from the lobby.

"Molly, could you cover the counter for a few minutes? I need to take a break." There were no windows in the lobby and, even if there had been, opening them wouldn't have lowered the sweltering temperature much. Ingrid had sweated off all her makeup, and her hair straggled in damp strands down the back of her neck. She was fanning her face with a folded fashion magazine. Molly felt sorry for her.

"Sure. Get something cold and plant yourself in front of a fan." She glanced at her wristwatch. It was only seven. Time seemed to drag when they weren't busy.

"I'm suffocating. Do you think Jude will close early tonight if they don't get the air conditioner fixed?"

"She might as well," Molly said. "I don't think we're going to have many more customers. Word about the breakdown must be out."

Ingrid plucked her limp blouse away from her damp breasts and headed for the kitchen. Molly leaned against the counter and fanned herself with the magazine Ingrid had left. The phone rang, and she reached for the receiver. It felt sticky in her hand.

"Hammond Motel and Restaurant."

"Is Mr. Delaney there?"

"Mr. Chet Delaney?"

"Uh, I don't know. I'm looking for somebody connected to Delaney Drilling Company."

"Well, Dirk Delaney, one of the partners, is in Houston. Chet Delaney is staying here, but he's out right now."

"Does the company have an office in Houston?"

"Yes. I can't give you the number, but I'm sure you can get it from Information."

"Okay. I want to talk to somebody about investing in an oil well. I owned a share of a well in that part of west Texas before. I bought it from an outfit called Petroleum Investors, but I haven't been able to get in touch with them by phone. All I have is a post office box, and my letters get nothing but the brush-off. I understand Delaney drilled the last hole I was in on. It came up dry, but I'm interested in making another investment."

Why are you telling me this? Molly wondered. "Do you want to leave a message for Chet Delaney?"

"Uh—no. I'll try Houston first. Thanks for the information." He'd hung up before Molly realized she hadn't even gotten his name.

Ingrid hurried down the hall just as Molly replaced the receiver. "We're closing," Ingrid said. "Jude just decided. The serviceman had to go to Snyder to get a compressor part. He probably won't get the air conditioner fixed before midnight." She locked the cash register, then pulled her purse from behind the counter. "I'm out of here."

"Me, too," Molly agreed, thinking of her cool bedroom. The air conditioner servicing the motel rooms was still operating.

She spent a few minutes helping Jude prepare the tables for the next morning's breakfast before retreating to her room, where she stripped and took a lukewarm shower. Then, donning panties and a bra, she stretched out on her bed and reached for the suspense novel she was halfway through. She had read only a paragraph when there was a knock at her door.

She scrambled up and pulled on her short, cotton robe, then opened the door, leaving the night chain engaged. "Yes?"

"Were you already in bed?" Chet grinned through the crack. "I didn't wake you, did I?"

"No, I was reading."

"I'm going out to the lake for a swim. Come with me?"

"Well..." Molly clutched the front of her robe together. She had to admit that a swim sounded like more fun than reading.

"It's early yet," he said.

Molly took a moment longer to consider the invitation before she said, "Okay. Give me a minute to get dressed."

"I'll meet you in the parking lot. It's too hot to stand around in this hallway."

Molly dug her faded blue bikini out of a drawer and put it on. She pulled on shorts and a knit shirt over it, then slid her feet into sandals, grabbed a towel and her keys, and let herself out.

Chet had pulled his car up to the motel's side entrance. He was sitting in the air-conditioned interior with the motor idling. Molly got in and buckled the safety belt as Chet pulled away from the motel.

"This is a terrific idea." She turned the air conditioner vent to let cool air blow on her face and rested the back of her head on the seat. "I needed to get out of there for a while."

"Rough day in the restaurant?" he asked, turning his head to study her.

"Not until the air conditioner conked out. After that it was pure hell. I've never been so hot in my life. And poor Ingrid. I actually thought she was going to keel over." Mentioning Ingrid reminded her of the phone call she'd taken. "By the way, a man called the motel for you about seven, while you were out."

"What man?"

"I didn't get his name, but I think it was a long-distance call. He asked for somebody connected to Delaney Drilling. When I said you were out and your uncle was in Houston, he decided to call Houston. I guess he'll call back if he doesn't get hold of your uncle."

"Did he say what he wanted?"

"Something about investing in an oil well. He said he'd bought a share in one of your wells that came up dry." She looked over at him. "It must have been the last one you drilled."

Chet's look sharpened. "It couldn't have been. We kept all the shares in that one, except for the landowner's customary one-sixteenth. Did he say it was in the Sunset field?"

Molly made an effort to recall everything the caller had said. "No, just that it was a Delaney well in west Texas."

"The Sunset's the only west Texas field we've drilled recently. It must have been a well we plugged some time back."

"I didn't get that impression," Molly mused. "He mentioned Petroleum Investors, said he'd bought the share through them."

"Never heard of them," Chet said. "The guy must be confused."

Molly had been vacillating about mentioning the letter she'd seen in the outgoing mail. But why shouldn't she? Surely there was nothing secret about it, since it had been tossed in the box for anyone to see who happened to look. She lifted her head from the seat and turned sideways as far as the seat belt would allow, facing Chet.

"This morning I checked the mailbox in the lobby to see if the mail had been delivered. It hadn't. Some outgoing letters were there, though. One of them was addressed to somebody in Maine, and 'Petroleum Investors, Inc.' was the name on the return address, with a post office box number in Fort Worth." Chet's quick glance was perplexed. "The Formbys are from Fort Worth, aren't they?"

"So are a lot of people. What are you trying to say, Molly?"

She raked her fingers through her hair. "I don't know. Is there anybody else at the motel who's from Fort Worth?"

"Not that I know of."

Molly settled back against the seat. "Maybe," she said, "the Formbys have some kind of business going on the side."

He was thoughtful for a moment. "They *have* formed a partnership, for tax purposes. They contract with independent companies like Delaney to supply experienced oil-field workers. Boney and the other guys working our well technically work for the Formbys, not Delaney. We pay the Formbys, and they pay the hands."

"But that doesn't have anything to do with investing."

"It's possible they've started a second company, I guess. People connected to the oil business are always starting little shoestring operations of one kind or another. That's how most of the major oil companies started. The Formbys might be picking up an oil lease here and there and selling shares." His eyes met hers briefly, and he frowned.

"What?"

"Something just occurred to me. A time or two in the past, our deal with the Formbys has included a share—usually one-quarter—in a well as part of their payment package. It reduces our cash outlay, and sometimes that's attractive. I don't know what they've done with their quarter shares, but they're free to keep them and hope for a producer, or go for the bird in the hand and sell them. I was under the impression, though, that we'd kept all the shares in both wells in the Sunset field."

"Don't you know?"

He expelled a breath. "Uncle Dirk handles our finances because he's in Houston and I'm in the field half the time. I know he had to do some fairly creative money-juggling to finance that first well without borrowing." He stared out at the highway for a few moments. "I never asked him for the details, but that phone call makes me wonder if he came up short and had to sign over a percentage to the Formbys in exchange for a reduction in their salaries."

"And the Formbys turned around and sold their percentage to the man who called you?"

"That's what I'm wondering."

"Wouldn't your uncle have told you?"

"Maybe not. He knew I was against parting with any shares beyond the landowner's." He made an ironic sound. "After studying Backus's early reports, I was so damned sure that well would produce." They were nearing the bridge that spanned the lake.

"Why don't you just ask David or Wilson if they received a share?"

"It might embarrass them to have to admit they turned right around and sold it. It doesn't matter now, anyway, but I'll ask Uncle Dirk about it the next time we talk."

He turned off the highway just before reaching the bridge, following a blacktop road. They drove for a few minutes in silence before they reached a lakeside picnic area, where a sandy bank sloped gently down to the water. Chet parked at the top of the incline and turned to her. She was deep in thought, and seemed unaware that they'd stopped.

"Molly?"

She stirred and turned her head toward him, then smiled a bit uncertainly.

"Let me guess. You're wondering what you're doing here with me."

She let out a long, shaky breath. "It's that obvious, huh?"

"To me."

Bowing her head, she released her safety belt. Wordlessly, he reached out and gathered her against him. Her arms came around him, but she didn't cling. All at once, he knew that he wanted more from her than a soft, responsive body against his or an eager mouth for tasting. He wanted to know her intimately—her mind and her feelings. Every part of her. He wanted her to share herself fully with him, and he wanted to give himself to her in return. He wanted to forget the conclusion he'd reached years ago, that he could not be who he was and make a relationship work.

He wanted too much, and it scared the hell out of him.

The depth of the tenderness that enveloped him was something new to him. Because of it, his hands were gentle as they half buried themselves in her hair.

Molly lifted her head and looked into his eyes. They were too much in shadow for her to read them, yet she sensed that if she could, she would find something there that she hadn't seen there before. He was not a man who lacked self-confidence, but he seemed hesitant now. What was he thinking? she wondered. What was he asking himself? With exquisite slowness, he lowered his head, and his lips touched hers.

The kiss was so careful, his mouth so soft, that it might have been the tentative kiss of an untried youth. His hands rested lightly on her as though he feared she would break if he applied any pressure. Molly sat quite still, simply accepting with wonder, and fearing that a movement or word from her would dispel the magic. She felt something opening inside her, a sweetness, an aching, that was deeper and more complicated than desire.

When he lifted his head, they stared at each other, perplexed and moved in a way that was new to both of them.

"I never know what to expect from you," she managed after a moment.

Chet turned away from her and opened the car door. "Let's have that swim now," he murmured.

Chapter 7

Carrying the old quilt from the trunk of the car, Chet followed her down the bank to the water, hanging back a little, shaken by the unfamiliar feelings that still lingered in him. What had happened in the car just now? he asked himself.

In the moonlight, she seemed an amorphous creature of fantasy, a figment of his imagination. She tugged her shirt over her head and stepped out of her shorts, then looked up the bank to where he'd stopped halfway down.

"Aren't you coming?"

"In a minute."

She hesitated an instant, looking up at him in silence, wondering why he had withdrawn from her. She felt unaccountably awkward all of a sudden. It was strange, she thought, how different everything seemed after the kiss in the car. On the drive out, conversation had been natural and easy. Now she could think of nothing to say that would not sound stilted and silly. Feeling ridiculous, she kicked off her sandals. "I'm going in," she said and ran to the water's edge.

Continuing down the slope, Chet unbuttoned his shirt and shrugged out of it. God, this was worse than his first date. What the hell was going on? he wondered, passing a frustrated hand through his hair. He watched her splashing in the shallow water, creating silver ripples on the water's moon-gilded surface.

She was like no other woman he'd ever known, and he had known a number in his thirty-two years. Since Molly had taken up residence in his mind, she'd driven all the others out. It was a dangerous state of affairs, yet he could not seem to get things back on safe footing again. All he had to do was stay away from her, right? So why had he asked her to come with him tonight? Because he needed to be with her?

Need. Yes, that was the word for what he felt. Not just want or desire. Even when he had the distinct feeling that she was merely tolerating his company in order to get answers to a curious array of questions ranging from the events surrounding the tragic death of George Backus to who held shares in Delaney drilled oil wells. He had never known a woman so inquisitive about things that should not have concerned her.

Yet she was concerned, or at least extremely interested, and when he asked her why, she said it was the mystery that intrigued her. He wanted to believe her. He told himself it made sense, since it was apparently Molly's uniqueness, her aura of mystery, that accounted for his finding her so irresistible.

On the other hand, if there was some hidden agenda behind all her questions, it would come out in due time. At the moment, he didn't want to think about it. He wanted to understand the dangerous need for her that he'd finally been honest enough to admit to himself. The fact that it had developed in such a short time made it even more alarming.

Thoughtfully, he dropped the quilt to the bank and removed his shoes, then unzipped his jeans and stripped them down over his swim trunks. Straightening, he stared at Molly. She was floating on her back, languidly moving her feet to keep herself afloat.

Something twisted in his stomach. Was he falling in love with her? Good God, that was a shocking thought. It couldn't be. Love was not in his plans, especially at this stage in his life. It was just the summer night and the sight of her near-naked body bathed in moonlight. He walked into the water and pushed himself away from the bank. It was like plunging into a dream. Tonight he would let the dream's current carry him. Tomorrow his head would be clearer.

Afloat on the water, staring up at thousands of blinking stars, Molly was assailed by the sudden remembrance that her father had died in the very water that felt so pleasantly soothing to her skin. Hot tears sprang to her eyes, blurring the stars overhead. She blinked them back as she heard Chet approaching.

She flipped over, and her feet found firm footing. The water was only breast-high. Tossing her wet hair back, she said, "I thought you'd changed your mind about a swim."

He rose from the water in front of her. Without a word, he reached out and drew her close. Sighing,

Molly felt the heat of tears in her eyes again. He had appeared when she was at her most vulnerable. Seeking comfort, she clung to him, pressing her face into the hollow of his neck. He smelled so good. His warm, wet flesh consoled her.

Murmuring her name, Chet ran a hand down her back with languid pleasure, to the place where her slick flesh was covered by her bikini bottom. Molly pressed against him, her hands gliding lazily over his back.

She made a throaty sound of pleasure and, tilting her head back, let her mouth trace the strong line of his jaw. He touched his lips to her forehead while his hand slipped beneath the bikini. As his mouth followed the curve of her cheek, tasting the faint saltiness of her skin, he groaned softly. He felt so heavy, and his movements were slow and easy and dreamlike.

His leg slid between hers and lifted to make intimate contact. She relaxed, and he supported her weight with his thigh as his lips began a leisurely journey over her face. With an inarticulate moan, she searched for his mouth with her own. When she found it, it was soft and hot and wet. He kissed her with slow, meticulous care.

This was not supposed to happen, whispered a small voice in Molly's head. She listened as though to a child's request, a child who doesn't know he's asking the impossible. Because the kiss in the car had changed everything, even if she didn't know why or how.

Dimly, she became aware that he was sliding her bikini bottom down, and she moved her legs to help him, wanting the freedom of nakedness, wanting to feel the water everywhere against her flesh.

Wanting to feel his body touching hers without barriers. She touched the top of his swimsuit, and then his hand was there helping her to peel it off and looping both suits over his arm. The dream carried them along.... The kiss lingered as they stroked and caressed each other beneath the water.

She is silk and fire, he thought, feeling a tug of desire. He undid the strap at the back of her neck, and her bikini top fell to her waist, still fastened by the second set of straps. Her breasts were free now, and he lifted one and sought the nipple with his mouth. It felt cool and hard in the night air.

Molly moaned and arched against him. He released the nipple to bring his mouth back to hers.

"Chet... Chet," she whispered against his lips, her hands moving over him with more urgency than before. Then she let her head fall back, as though she no longer had the strength to hold it upright, and he pressed soft, wet kisses along her throat.

Then he brought his mouth back to her breast to nibble and stroke with his tongue. He could hear her breathing faster, almost as fast as he, and dimly he was aware of her fingernails digging into his back. When his mouth moved a little higher, he could feel her heartbeat pumping against his lips.

Suddenly passion was a ball of fire in his stomach.

He gripped her buttocks with both hands and brought her lower body hard against his. Her hips moved with a rhythm as old as the human race. She murmured something that he could not understand, could barely hear above the roaring in his ears. For an instant his saner self surfaced, and he tried to shake the fog from his head and claw his way out of the dream, but the rhythmic movement of their bodies seduced him back. It was so easy to slip inside her.

Then he no longer knew what was dream and what was reality. There was only Molly and the driving demands of his body, and they filled his world.

The sultry night air dried Molly's skin quickly. Leafy tree branches reached black, shadowy fingers out over the bank and blotted out the stars. Chet had carried her from the water, laying her on the thin quilt he'd brought from his car. Even though the night was oppressively warm, she shuddered as she emerged from the dreamlike state that had enveloped her since their arrival at the lake. His warm arm drew her closer to his hard, hot flesh.

She was nestled against Chet's side, her head resting on his chest. She could feel the racing thump of his heart against her cheek and hear his still unsteady breathing. His skin was drying quickly, like hers. His hand rested on her wet hair, his fingers laced between the strands. The taste of him remained in her mouth, treacherously sweet and seductive. Images of the two of them making love in the water crept slowly into her sluggish mind, as though struggling through thick, sweet syrup. Her flesh still hummed with the memory of his touch.

She wished she could remain swaddled in her trancelike state, buffered from reality. But with the slowing of her heart and the cooling of her flesh, her brain cleared. Reality was harsh and unforgiving.

With a sound of despair, she struggled to a sitting position, tugging the corner of the quilt around her. "What have we done?"

Still heavy and dazed, Chet opened his eyes to peer at her. Her face was dimly visible, and he could make out the faint gleam of her eyes. She was hugging her bent knees and clutching the edges of the quilt. "What kind of question is that?"

"I didn't come out here with you to—to have sex." It had been more than having sex, so much more, but she couldn't bring herself to label it accurately.

His body still leaden and throbbing, he was as shaken as she. He dragged himself up on his elbow and raked a hand through his damp hair. "Molly..."

"I can't understand how it happened," she said, fumbling to remove her wet bikini top beneath the quilt. Then she felt around for her shirt. Finding it, she let the quilt drop away as she jerked the shirt over her head.

He watched her in bewilderment. "Do you think I planned it?" he asked blankly.

"I don't know," she said unhappily. "Did you?"

He rubbed a hand over his face. "Good God, no."

"I can't believe both of us lost our heads," Molly said bitterly. "*One* of us should have stopped it."

"Meaning me?" Chet watched her stand and struggle into her shorts. Why was she trying to make him totally responsible for what had happened? The injustice of it made his temper rise. He pushed himself up and grabbed his jeans, tugged them on. "You weren't exactly a teenage virgin, Molly."

"*I* seduced *you?*" she demanded. "Is that what you're saying? That's cruel, and it's not true, Chet Delaney. I despise you!" She sat and tried to see through angry tears in order to buckle her sandals.

He fought off the urge to shake her. "You thought I was anything but cruel a few minutes ago," he retorted. "You couldn't get enough of me."

Pain shot through her finger as she stabbed it with the sharp point of a buckle. Oh, yes, she had ground herself against him like a sex-starved nymphomaniac, and he had been warm and tender, eager to give her what her body begged for. He was dead right, but that only added to her humiliation. "That doesn't mean I have to be happy about it!"

"Happy?" he responded. "No, I don't guess either of us is happy about it. Damn it, Molly, I'm as appalled as you are!" He fought down a sensation of angry confusion as he grabbed his shirt and pulled it on, then his shoes, jerking and tying the laces with more force than was necessary.

He was shocked to discover that guilt was among the confusion of feelings battling inside him. He'd never suffered that particular emotion because of a woman before. All his women had been more than willing. Molly had been willing, too, so why the hell should he feel guilty? Somehow he felt that he should have sensed doubt in her response, but, damn it, there hadn't been any until afterward. He still felt faintly ashamed, and he didn't know how to deal with it.

"I'm not a person who loses control," she said finally in a low voice. "I don't like it."

"Join the club," he muttered when he'd gained some measure of composure. He finished tying his shoes and rose. "Let's face it, Molly, we're two consenting adults."

She wished he wouldn't keep shoving the truth into her face. It frightened her. "Consent assumes there was some discussion and understanding beforehand."

"Discussion." He laughed harshly. "You don't discuss something like that. You sure as hell can't understand it."

"So we'll just have to put it down to a fever of the brain," she snapped.

"Something like that," he muttered. "The question is, what do we do now?"

"Do?" she asked blankly. "All I want to do is go back to the motel. And to my room. Alone." She snatched up her wet bikini and brushed past him, starting up the slope to the car. He grabbed his suit and the quilt and followed.

A heavy silence filled the car on the drive back to town. In his bewildered anger, Chet stubbornly waited for her to speak. Even if she blamed him, hearing about it would be better than the strained silence, which seemed more accusing than words.

He held out until they reached the motel, but as soon as he'd parked, he turned to her and said, "We're going to have to deal with it, Molly."

She stared at him. Did he want to dissect every detail of what had happened? She couldn't bear that. How could he expect it of her? "I think we should just forget it."

"Oh, that'll work," he mocked. "Why didn't *I* think of that?"

"There's no need for sarcasm, Chet," she said stiffly.

"Then don't pretend you can forget what happened. You can't—any more than I can," he said with deceptive softness. He got out of the car and slammed the door. Then he slapped a palm down on the hood of the car, stared out at the street and cursed in helpless frustration.

Molly scrambled out, stalked across the parking lot and entered the motel.

In her room, she threw her wet bikini against a wall and fell across the bed without even turning on the light. She clutched the spread in both hands, burying her face between them. He was mad, she told herself. They both were.

There was only one reason for her to be in this godforsaken place, and he'd made her forget it. Made her forget everything. The lies-by-omission that she'd told Jude, whom she'd come to like and admire. Taking advantage of Lauren's childish trust to mine for information about her father. Exploiting her new friendship with Wilson Formby. She'd even forgotten her father's death and the general acceptance that he'd killed himself by driving while intoxicated. But it wasn't true, she thought fiercely.

A choked sob escaped her and was muffled by the bedspread. It wasn't true! Chet had made her forget that. She'd had every intention of going for a swim, asking more questions about her father and returning to the motel, having gotten him to drop his guard a little more with her. Instead, she felt betrayed. He'd dropped his guard, all right, but so had she. He'd made her feel cherished, desirable, alive. He'd made her forget her father's last letter, written when he had less than twenty-four hours left to live.

The Delaneys are up to something.

She turned her head to the side and stared into the darkness, relaxing her grip on the spread. How could tonight have happened with a man she'd known so briefly? A man who might harbor guilty knowledge about her father's last days of life?

No. Chet could not be culpable, her heart cried. Not the man who had made love to her with such gentleness and care. Not the man who had wooed her into such sweet surrender.

She closed her eyes and bit down on her lip. No, she could not believe it of Chet. He had never treated her dishonorably. Alone in the darkness, she could admit it. Chet had been no more to blame for what had happened tonight than she had. Hadn't she reached for him at the same moment that he had reached for her? Hadn't she clung to him, drawing heart-pounding pleasure from pressing her body against his? Hadn't she reveled dreamily in touching him, cooperated fully in ridding them both of their swimsuits, marveled at the rightness of having him inside her?

She had been neither unconscious nor hypnotized. Nor had she been seduced. She had known exactly what was going to happen from the moment he'd kissed her in the car, and she had done nothing to stop it. She had wanted to put the blame on him because she was terrified of dealing with her own feelings.

Closing her eyes again, she pressed her fingers against the bridge of her nose. Her father must have been wrong, or partly so. There were two Delaneys. And from what Chet had said tonight, Dirk Delaney sometimes made business decisions and acted on them without informing Chet. For one thing, he might have given the Formby brothers a share of the previous Delaney well and kept it from his nephew.

Chet didn't seem disturbed by the possibility. It was apparently a legitimate business practice and, if his uncle had done it, it had been a judgment call and nobody had been hurt by it.

But if Dirk Delaney would sign over a share of a well to outsiders without getting Chet's agreement, he might also make other, less-than-legitimate decisions without Chet's knowledge. Chet had as much as admitted that Delaney Drilling was in a financial bind, and Dirk Delaney had spent his life developing the company from a tiny, shoestring operation to a multimillion-dollar business. How far would he go to keep it from going under? Beyond the boundaries of the law? And if he had, and her father had discovered it, had he committed a worse crime to protect himself?

But what crime? Witnesses had said her father was staggering when he got into his car that day. Could he have been drinking alcohol—vodka—without knowing it? It could have been added to whatever he was drinking that day, and the half-empty bottle of whiskey planted to make it look as though George Backus had been sneaking straight shots on the job. Anyone at the site that day could probably have done it, and Dirk Delaney had been there. But he couldn't have been sure that her father would lose control of the car, or, if he did, that he would die as a result.

And how on earth was she to learn the truth about any of these speculations?

Turning over, she pushed her tangled, still damp hair away from her face and stared at the black outlines of the chest and the rocking chair beside it. The little room seemed so barren suddenly, so lonely.

What was she going to do now? she wondered. Straighten things out with Chet? The thought made her want to squirm. But she knew it had to be done. She had been a full participant in the night's debacle, and if there was blame to be laid, she would accept her share. They had to deal with it, he'd said. She was curious to know how he thought they could accomplish that.

Chapter 8

Molly rinsed out her bikini, which had lain crumpled in a corner of her room all night, and draped it over the shower rod.

Bracing her hands on the washbasin, she stared at her crumpled shirt in the mirror above the bowl. She had awakened early and had been momentarily disoriented when she discovered she'd slept in her clothes. Then the events of the previous night had flooded into her mind. She would have preferred to go back to sleep so she wouldn't have to deal with reality.

She had slept deeply, and if she'd had dreams, she couldn't remember them. Which was probably just as well, she thought unhappily, since her dreams would undoubtedly have included Chet.

A wrinkle in her pillowcase had left a line across one cheek. She rubbed halfheartedly at the mark with the tip of a finger, then turned away from her reflection.

She showered, dressed in slacks and a shirt for the workday, and applied a dash of makeup and lip gloss.

Even then, it was only seven-thirty, too early for breakfast. She found the novel she'd been reading and settled in the rocker with it. But the suspenseful story didn't hold her attention, and after a few minutes she dropped the book on the floor beside the chair. What was happening in her own life was so intrusive that fiction couldn't compete.

Rising, she paced the cramped little room, caught between anxiety and annoyance over what had happened the night before. The intervening hours should have given her some distance, she told herself. She ought to be able to approach the problem more calmly. She couldn't afford to spend her time in Sunset being torn up inside; her purpose in being there was too important.

She started for the door, but as quickly reversed her direction. She would have to face Chet sooner or later, but it didn't have to be this morning. She couldn't lie to herself. She still felt raw and vulnerable. She would go in for breakfast later, after he'd left for the well site, if she decided to have breakfast at all. The thought of food brought the discovery that she felt faintly nauseated.

Impatient with herself, she pictured Chet enjoying a hearty working man's breakfast. The picture irritated her as the queasiness in her own stomach stirred uncomfortably.

Good Lord, she hadn't felt like this since she was sixteen and madly infatuated with a boy in her science class. Whenever he spoke to her, even if it was only to ask if he could borrow a pencil, she'd been struck dumb. Looking back on it, it seemed that she'd been nauseated and unable to eat for most of her junior year.

Well, she wasn't sixteen now, she told herself, as she paced across the room again. Finding herself in front of the bureau, she opened the top drawer and took out the envelope containing her father's last letter. She drew out the folded pages and dropped the envelope on top of the dresser. Returning to her restless walking, she unfolded the letter and read.

Dear Lala...can't wait 'til you get here...I've arranged to rent a ski rig for your visit...a strange undercurrent here...the Delaneys are up to something.

Tears of frustration filled her eyes as she refolded the pages. Would she ever know what her father had really meant by those last lines? Angrily, she wiped her eyes with the back of her hand.

Then she heard footsteps and a tap at her door. "Molly?" It was Chet.

Furtively, she stuffed the letter into her pocket, as though he could see her. Bowing to the inevitable, she opened the door.

"Yes?" she inquired softly.

He squinted at her through the narrow opening. "I wanted to check on your before I left for work. Are you okay?"

Her intended apology, carefully reasoned out the night before, was overruled by his assumption that last night had made such an impact on her that she needed checking up on.

"I'm fine. Perfect."

Without waiting for an invitation, he brushed past her and into the room. She closed the door, leaned back against it, arms folded, and waited.

"You're still upset," he said.

It was difficult to remain indignant as she took in his desolate expression. This wasn't easy for him, either. "I'm fine. Really."

He dropped into the rocker and absently picked up her novel, glanced at the cover and dropped it to the floor again. His gaze, when he turned it on her, would have been mild had his eyes not been so darkly intense. "You don't look fine."

"What a flatterer," she said, cocking her head to one side. The words elicited no smile. "What do you want from me, Chet?"

"How about honesty?"

With a helpless sound, Molly pushed herself away from the door and slumped down on the side of the bed. "Honesty? About what?"

"Damn it, Molly, I'm trying to sort out my feelings about what happened."

Wearily she dragged a hand through her hair. "I can't even sort out my own feelings. All I know is that it was a disastrous mistake."

Restlessly Chet rose from the rocker. He stared at her for a moment, as though wondering if he should take the few steps that separated them. Her body and her mind tensed, whatever emotional distance the night had given her gone. *Don't let him touch me!*

Abruptly he moved to the bureau and leaned against it, his arm resting along its top. He appeared relaxed, except that his fingers gripped the edge until his knuckles were white.

"A mistake. Okay, we agree on one thing. So how come we can't put it out of our minds? How come we're both so miserable?"

Molly wanted to scream. Why was he so intent on stripping away all her defenses? A dull throbbing had begun behind her eyes. She pressed the heel of her hand against her temple. "Speak for yourself, damn you!" The next instant, she regretted her outburst. She sighed and rubbed the bridge of her nose. "I don't know why you have to pick it to pieces. It just makes it worse. My God, I thought only women were guilty of that kind of hashing and rehashing."

He released his grip on the bureau, looking as though he wanted to kick something. But he remained still, the wounded flicker in his eyes quickly controlled. He picked up the envelope lying near his arm and glanced at it idly. "You," he said grimly, tapping the corner of the envelope on the bureau to punctuate his words, "are terrified of facing your feelings."

"Thank you for that thumbnail analysis, Dr. Delaney!" She leaped from the bed as the chill in his eyes turned to fire. Then her gaze flew to the envelope he still held in his hand, and, suddenly, her frustration gave way to something far more frightening. He had picked up the envelope addressed to her, in her father's writing!

Panicked, she lunged for the envelope and tore it from his fingers. "Give me that! Who do you think you are? Do you think last night gives you the right to march in here and read my mail?" She crushed the envelope in a shaking hand and crammed it into her pocket with the letter.

He stared at her in astonishment, and a muscle in his jaw hardened. "Good question," he retorted. "Exactly what rights *does* last night give me?"

"Let me lay it out for you," she snapped. "Zero. Zilch. Last night I accepted an invitation to go for a swim. That's what I expected to do. *All* I expected to do. Until you started your little campaign!"

"What little campaign was that?" he asked silkily.

"Kissing me until—until I couldn't think and—" The final hold over her temper snapped. "Oh, to hell with it! And you!" She deliberately turned her back on him. She would not break down in front of him. She wished he would just go and leave her in peace.

Pushed beyond his ability to control himself, Chet spun her around again and grabbed her shoulders. "Stop it, Molly! No campaign was necessary. Do you hear me? You agreed to go. You kissed me, too. You could have said no at any point, but you were hungry for it. You want me this very minute. You can't help yourself any more than I can."

Eyes wide with outrage, Molly pulled free of his grasp. "You're a liar!"

"Is that a fact?" he demanded.

"Yes!"

With a swift move, Chet hauled her back into his arms and kissed her savagely. Furious, she tried to protest, but her angry words were muffled by his mouth, and he crushed her harder against him.

After a brief moment she stopped struggling and relaxed against him with a moan. He took the kiss deeper, congratulating himself on proving his point. He wanted to slam her need in her face so hard that she could never deny it again. He wanted to take out his anger and frustration on her. And then he simply wanted her, needed her more desperately than he'd ever needed anything.

He wrenched his mouth from hers with an oath of self-disgust. Gasping for breath, they stared at each other. In that moment, Molly knew unequivocally that she loved him.

Her whole body throbbed with desire. A small part of her still wanted to deny it, to break away from him, to flee. But it was no match for the other part of her that was pure need, raging to be acknowledged and satisfied. When she did move, it wasn't away from him. Instead, she clasped his head in her hands and greedily sought his mouth with a muffled cry of surrender.

There was nothing of the dreamlike quality of the previous night's lovemaking. This was demand, greed, possession. They were ravenous for each other. Mouths and bodies fused together, they fell across the bed, already fumbling at unwanted clothing, peeling it away from flesh that was hot and throbbing.

Starved for the feel of him, Molly ran her hands over the muscles in his back, the hardness of his lean flanks, the rough hairs on his chest, purring with pleasure. Once the avalanche of passion broke, she could hold nothing back. Frantic for more, she shifted atop him and moved her head to gain deeper access to his hot, avid mouth.

She felt as though she would explode with wanting him. She thrust her tongue into his mouth and nipped fretfully at his bottom lip. Chet groaned and rolled her over, pulling her back from the edge of the narrow bed and lying, full length, atop her. The hardness of his need throbbed against her stomach, sending a wild thrill through her. Clutching two handfuls of his hair, she murmured his name again and again in a mindless chant of incoherent longing.

Driven beyond thought, Chet crushed his open mouth to hers and thrust into her. She responded by arching hard against him in a silent plea for more. It drove him to the edge of madness.

As quick as lightning, Molly felt the fire gathering in her belly, and she pressed him closer. The sounds of their ragged breathing filled the room. Dimly, she was aware that, had she been herself, she would have been appalled by such a fierce and savage coupling. But she was not herself. She had become some wild, daring creature that she didn't recognize, and she reveled in it.

The fire in her belly was molten liquid now, threatening to burn her alive. Then it boiled up out of its pit, and the undulating waves began to spread from her belly throughout her body with an exquisite pain-pleasure that was almost too much to bear. She wanted the waves of fire to stop before they destroyed her, and she wanted them to go on and on without end.

She was foggily aware when Chet stiffened and cried out, and then he collapsed against her with a gasp that became a groan of staggering release. He was so heavy that she could barely breathe, yet she wrapped her arms round him, not wanting to move.

Her skin was wet, and her eyelids felt as if they were made of lead. Replete, her body no longer clamored for more. She felt as though she'd been picked up by a hurricane, shaken and battered to the limit of endurance, then dropped on a peaceful shore.

She was drifting toward a sated sleep when Chet stirred and shifted his weight off her. Dragging her eyes open, she found him watching her, his head propped up on his hand, his eyes bemused.

She smiled lazily and ran a hand slowly down his shoulder to flatten it against his chest. She could feel his heart pounding against her palm. So vital, she thought with a tingle of pleasure. He was so vitally male, such a reckless, demanding lover. Her body hummed with contentment in every pore. Her eyes drifted closed again.

He trailed a finger down her cheek. "Molly..." She opened her eyes to find him still staring at her, a small frown between his brows. "I didn't come here for this. Please believe me."

"Shh," she murmured and turned her head so that her lips pressed against his upper arm. "I do believe you." She gazed up at him. "Things didn't exactly go as I'd planned, either." She spread her fingers over his back, feeling as though she would never get enough of simply touching him. "I fully intended to apologize for the things I said last night. I was every bit as responsible as you for what happened. I just hated to admit it. Then, when you came, all I could do was accuse you again. It was easier."

With a deep sigh, he combed his fingers through her hair, laying his hand along her cheek. "I thought that was what I wanted to hear, but it doesn't really change anything."

He sounded so forlorn. She looked at him gravely. "How would you like things to change?"

He gave a quiet, humorless laugh and rubbed the pad of his thumb lightly along the line of one dark, arched brow. "I don't know," he said cautiously. "I've always been able to be with a woman and then go away from her when the time came without leaving any-thing of myself behind. But it's never been quite the same as it is with you. I'm afraid of how much I want you. I'm not sure what's going on here."

She gave a quiet laugh and pressed her face into his shoulder. "Don't look to me for the answer. I'm as confused as you are."

He touched her hair, brushed a soft kiss across her brow. "I don't want either of us to get hurt."

She wanted to say that it was already too late. She loved him, and love could cause the worst hurt of all. Especially if it turned out that she'd been wrong in be-lieving he hadn't contributed to her father's death. That would be a hurt from which she would never re-cover.

But he couldn't have. If she hadn't felt that in her bones, she couldn't have given herself to him so com-pletely. "It would be wonderful if someone could guarantee that neither of us will get hurt, but life isn't like that. We just have to stumble through it as best we can."

Fighting back a need to gather her into his arms and start making love to her all over again, Chet kissed her lips lightly. "I guess you're right." Then he kissed her again, lingeringly this time. "If I don't get up right now, I won't be at work for another two hours." With an enormous effort of will, he rolled off the bed and began untangling his clothes from hers.

Molly drew her knees up and hugged the pillow, watching him dress. She loved the way the muscles in his back and arms rippled when he moved, and the stark contrast between his sunbronzed arms, face and neck, and the paler part of his body. He was incredibly exciting to her.

He finished tucking in his shirt and sat on the side of the bed to put on his shoes. When he was done, he let his gaze linger for a long moment on the bare curve of her hip and the smooth line of her thigh. Then he sighed and bent to taste once more of her kiss-bruised mouth.

"You're so beautiful," he murmured. He rose abruptly then, as if to shake off a spell. "Would you like to go for a drive this evening?"

He put the question casually. No strings. He'd made that plain. She replied in the same careless tone. "I'll have to wait and see how tired I am."

"Okay." He stood, averting his eyes from the creamy satin-smooth skin that beckoned to him to return to bed and to hell with work.

He hesitated, wanting to say something else, something reassuring, but not finding the right words. He couldn't remember ever suffering from so much uncertainty and self-doubt. He felt as though his whole life had been turned upside down and settled into an entirely new pattern. "See you later."

When he was gone, the room felt empty. But, except for her father, she'd been alone for a long time. She had learned to deal with it, she told herself.

She stretched and yawned and snuggled up to the pillow, where Chet's scent still lingered. Breathing it in, she closed her eyes and drifted into sleep.

Continuing to feel distracted, Chet worked until after noon, concentrating on soil samples and seismograph logs and drill tests to steer his mind away from questions for which he had no answers. Finally, tiring of the struggle, he pushed aside the logs he'd been studying and got up to brew fresh coffee to go with his lunch.

When the coffee was ready, he poured a cup and set it on the floor next to the sofa while he opened his lunch bucket. Elsie had packed ham-and-cheese sandwiches, a slab of carrot cake and a giant red apple.

Barely aware of what he was eating, he looked around at the interior of the trailer where he'd worked for the past two months, as though seeing it for the first time. Everything in his life had changed, it seemed. But not really. The change was in himself, though he wasn't sure what it meant or what would come of it. He was used to knowing where he was going, being in control, and this uncertainty disturbed him.

Sitting back on the couch, he relived his visit to Molly's room that morning. He hadn't gone there with the intention of making love to her, he insisted to himself. Not that he hadn't wanted to the instant he saw her. He chuckled ruefully, remembering how she'd looked at him with those big gray eyes. Those eyes had wanted him, and she'd tried to deny it by picking a fight. Accused him of reading her mail.

He frowned as he recalled how she'd snatched that envelope away from him. Almost as if she had something to hide. He closed his eyes and tried to see the envelope again. He'd scanned it when he picked it up, but he hadn't really been paying attention. He'd been fully occupied with fighting himself to keep from grabbing Molly and losing himself in her body.

So, he mused with a sigh, he'd lost that battle.

His mind went back to the envelope. He remembered thinking there was something odd about it. He concentrated on bringing its image into focus behind his closed eyelids. He could see it. It had been addressed to Molly at her former address in Dallas. Nothing particularly odd about that. The letter it contained must have been important to her, since she'd brought it to Sunset with her. He wondered briefly if it was from her ex-husband.

No, that didn't feel right. Think, he ordered himself. What else was there on the envelope? A return address? That was it! Suddenly he could see it as clearly as he had in Molly's room. There had been no name in the upper left hand corner of the envelope, but the return address had been the Hammond Motel, Sunset, Texas.

Now, how could Molly have had a letter mailed to her from somebody in Sunset while she was still in Dallas? She hadn't known anyone in Sunset before her arrival.

He shook his head and tried to make some sense of it. He had a feeling that the handwriting on the envelope had seemed vaguely familiar. Where had he seen it before?

All at once, his mind made a staggering connection. No, he told himself. Impossible.

He jumped up from the sofa and opened a drawer beneath the work counter, then lifted out a file folder jammed with reports and papers and began rifling through them, scanning and discarding them, one after the other, until they were scattered haphazardly over the counter.

Near the back of the folder, he found what he'd been looking for. He stared at the typed report, dropping his gaze to the signature at the bottom. He couldn't be sure. But maybe his crazy flash of insight wasn't impossible after all.

He dropped the report with the others on the counter and slammed out of the trailer. On the drive to town, he forced himself to stay within the speed limit and to think through what he was going to do with reasonable calm.

By the time he reached the gas station on the west edge of town, he'd figured out where to start. With Jude Hammond. But if he went to the motel, he would have to face Molly, and he wasn't ready for that yet. Not until he knew. He went into the gas station and used the pay phone to call Jude.

"Hi, Chet, what can I do for you?"

"I've been doing some housecleaning out at the site, culling old files. I found some personal papers left by George Backus. They're probably not important, but I thought I'd bundle them up and sent them to his family anyway. Didn't you say he had a daughter?"

"Yeah," Jude replied. "She's in Dallas, I think."

"Would you happen to have her name and address?"

"Gee, I'm sorry, Chet, but I can't help you. All I ever heard him call her was Lala."

"What did you do with his clothes, after the accident?"

"Let me think." Chet ran an impatient hand through his hair as he waited for Jude to mull it over. "Wait a minute—I remember now. I looked through his wallet for one of those cards telling you who to notify in case of an accident, you know?"

"And?"

"He didn't have one. I knew he'd received letters from his daughter, but I couldn't find those, either. He must have thrown them away after he read them. I think there were some snapshots but I didn't really look at them...."

Chet struggled to hang on to his patience. "The clothes, Jude?" he prompted.

"Oh, yeah. Well, I didn't know what to do. But Elsie suggested I box up all his stuff and send it over to the funeral home. Since the body was there, we figured the daughter or somebody would be contacting them, and they could get the address where to send George's things. I seem to remember the funeral home people saying the police here had contacted the Dallas police, who traced George's daughter through his neighbors. I guess that's how she learned about the accident, and the police probably put her in touch with the funeral home."

"Thanks, Jude. You've been a big help." Chet hung up and hurried back to his car.

Curled in the rocker in her room, Molly was spending her afternoon break doing absolutely nothing. Her head resting against the chair's high back, she rocked slowly and wondered what Chet was doing at that moment. Writing a report? Eating lunch? Talking with Wilson or Boney? She had been unable to think of anything but him all morning. It had made her so absentminded that she'd mixed up two orders and, after straightening that out, instructed Elsie to cook a burger well-done when the customer had ordered rare.

"Where's your mind today?" Jude had asked when Molly took the well-done burger back to exchange it for another, cooked according to order.

"I think I'm coming down with something," she had stammered, and felt Jude and Elsie studying her curiously as she left the kitchen.

She had to get her act together before her evening shift, she told herself. Maybe a nap would help. She closed her eyes and settled more comfortably in the chair.

She was nearly asleep a few minutes later when somebody banged loudly on her door. She almost leaped out of her skin. "Hold your horses," she muttered crossly as she uncurled herself.

The caller banged again, as though trying to break the door in. She reached the door and slid the night chain from its lock. "I'm coming!"

Before she could turn the knob, there was more insistent pounding. Molly gave an angry jerk and opened the door. "I said I'm—"

Giving her a none-too-gentle shove, Chet removed her from his path and stormed into the room. "Shut the door," he ordered.

"Don't tell me what to do!"

With a curse, Chet whipped around her and slammed the door. Molly watched, openmouthed, as he circled the rocker and gripped the high back with both hands. She had the distinct impression that he wanted to throw it across the room.

"Chet, what in the world—"

"I've just come from the funeral home."

The deadly fury in his eyes was enough to make her gasp in alarm. "Have you lost your mind? What are you talking about?"

"I've had enough of your playacting," he shot back. So furious he could barely contain himself, he kept his fingers clamped to the chair back to keep them from finding their way around her lovely neck. Never in all his life had he felt so betrayed. "I don't know what your game is, Molly *Backus* Sinclair," he shouted, "but I intend to find out before I leave here."

Molly felt the blood leave her face. She had to grab hold of the bedpost to steady herself. He'd come from the funeral home, he'd said. The funeral home where she'd made arrangements to have her father's body and belongings shipped home. She didn't know what had made him go there, but it didn't matter now. He would have had to know eventually, but not like this. Oh God, not like this....

She sank down on the bed and buried her face in her hands for a moment. Everything was a mess. She'd failed miserably at investigating her father's death. She'd fallen in love with Chet, and he might never forgive her for deceiving him. Yet she'd had no choice but to play things exactly as she had. She wouldn't apologize for trying to discover the truth about her father's last days. She wouldn't!

When she'd composed herself enough to speak, she looked up and said defiantly, "George Backus was my father, and I knew him better than anyone."

"That much I know," he ground out. "What I don't know is what the hell you think you're doing in Sunset."

"I had to find out the truth."

He looked at her blankly.

"My father had no reason to start drinking again." She took a deep breath and forced herself to go on. "Unless...well, unless he knew something that was dangerous to somebody. I don't know what really happened, but I don't believe his death was an accident."

Chet stared at her, thunderstruck. After a long moment of paralyzed silence, he released his grip on the chair and let his hands fall to his sides, as though they were too heavy to hold up any longer. "Good God, Molly, what are you saying?"

She felt herself wavering in the face of his shock, but there was no going back now. "He—he wrote to me the day before he died. He said he thought something strange was going on at the well site."

Chet was pacing restlessly in front of the closet now, back and forth, back and forth. The envelope she'd snatched from him had contained the letter from her father. Had Backus been drunk when he wrote it?

"He—" Molly looked down at her hands "—well, he said he thought the Delaneys were up to something."

Chet halted in his tracks to glare at her.

She rushed on, "If he did turn to alcohol, it was because he was worried about something at work."

"Are you suggesting that *I* had something to do with your father's starting to drink again?"

She looked up at him, her eyes full of questions and doubts. "No, I—I don't know what he meant when he wrote that about you and your uncle. But I won't be satisfied until I find out the truth, whatever it is. You must know something that would help me, Chet, if you'll only think about it."

"This is unbelievable! God, I feel like such a fool. You went to bed with me because you think I know something and you thought that would loosen my tongue!"

"No!" Molly cried. "You can't possibly believe that!" She swallowed convulsively. "It's ironic. I *fought* myself to keep from making love with you. I didn't want emotions getting in the way."

He dragged a hand through his hair in a gesture that bespoke more clearly than words his utter frustration. Then he stuffed both hands into his trouser pockets and shook his head in dismay. "Molly, you're kidding yourself. You want to believe your father didn't fall off the wagon. Maybe you have to, I don't know. But there were witnesses. Why would the men say your father was drunk if he wasn't?"

She lifted her shoulders in a helpless shrug. "I don't know. It's just that something doesn't feel right. I can't be more precise than that."

His anger was draining out of him, being replaced by a feeling of futility. How could you reason with a feeling? How could you explain away a daughter's stubborn refusal to see her father as frail and flawed? "I don't know what else to say to you."

"There's nothing more to say. But there's something you *can* do. You can help me find out what really happened."

He pressed his thumb and forefinger against the bridge of his nose and closed his eyes for an instant, but no answers came to him. He paced the width of the room again, wondering if she could possibly be right.

She was so damned adamant. But people could be adamant and wrong at the same time. "Does anyone else in Sunset know who you really are?"

"No, they couldn't. I haven't told anyone."

He paced and stared at his feet for another few moments. "Just out of curiosity," he said finally, "how long has it been since your divorce?"

"Six years."

He made a sound in his throat. "I've been laboring under the impression that it was recent, that you'd left Dallas to get away from him."

"I rarely think of him anymore. Sometimes I can't believe I was ever married."

He looked at her for a long, thoughtful moment. "Did you really give up your job in Dallas to go on this wild-goose chase?"

"No," she murmured. "I'm a guidance counselor in the public school system. I'm on my two-month summer vacation."

"Great," he muttered. "Wait 'til Jude hears this."

"I feel terrible about deceiving her, but I couldn't have stayed here at the motel without taking the waitress job. Are you going to tell her?"

He studied her for a moment, then shook his head. "I think we should keep this between us for now." He went to the door. "I have to get out of here and think."

He still looked grim, but Molly felt the tight dread in her chest loosening. "Does this mean you're starting to believe me?"

He turned back to her. "No, Molly, it doesn't. But I'd rather be safe than sorry." He opened the door and went out, closing it behind him.

I don't care what he says, she told herself. He's not sure I'm wrong or he wouldn't have said we should keep quiet about my father. Heaving a sigh, she flopped back across the bed and stared at the ceiling. A treacherous thought crept into her mind. She tried to shoo it out, but it wouldn't go.

She couldn't help wondering if Chet had his own private reasons for wanting to keep her identity a secret.

Chapter 9

Chet returned to the well site, but he might as well have stayed at the motel. He was too stunned and confused to work. Merely thinking didn't accomplish much, either, though he did plenty of that as he sat alone in the trailer. He didn't return to the motel until dark. After dinner, he told Molly he wasn't up to going out. He was bushed and needed to get some sleep. Besides, he'd be rotten company in the mood he was in.

She accepted his words without comment. He did look tired, but she suspected that he didn't want to be with her, in any case. He'd discovered she wasn't who he'd thought she was, and maybe that would make a crucial difference in their relationship.

What *was* their relationship, anyway? she wondered as she moved about the restaurant, waiting on late customers. She didn't even know how he felt about her—especially now. He had never spoken of love. It wasn't his fault that she'd fallen in love with him. He'd asked for no commitments, given no promises. He'd made it clear from the beginning that he had a low opinion of marriage.

Marriage. She couldn't even let herself think the word. Marriage meant trust, and how could Chet ever trust her now?

So she would stop thinking about love, she told herself as she cleared the dirty dishes from a table. She had fallen in love, and she could fall back out of it again. She had done it with Tom, hadn't she? But Chet's nothing like Tom, a small voice in her head protested. Tom was shallow, selfish, immature. Chet was . . .

Her mind was getting clouded with emotion. Frightened, Molly forced it away. Emotion had landed her in the mess she was in. It wasn't what she needed to get her out of it.

After the restaurant closed, she set up the tables for breakfast alone. Lauren had come down with a cold, and Jude, who had spent the evening running back and forth from the restaurant to the apartment to check on her daughter, had finally accepted Molly's repeated offers to take care of things in the restaurant and stayed with Lauren.

Ingrid left at nine-fifteen, Elsie a few minutes later. Molly didn't mind having the place to herself as she spread clean tablecloths and placed folded napkins on the tables. She wasn't in a communicative mood.

At nine-thirty she finished and made one last circuit of the dining room to assure herself that she hadn't forgotten anything. As she left the dining room, the telephone in the lobby rang. Jude had an extension in her apartment, but Molly grabbed the receiver anyway. If the call was for one of the guests, Jude wouldn't have to be disturbed.

"Yes?"

"Hello? Is this the Hammond Motel?"

"Yes, it is. This is Molly Sinclair speaking. May I help you?"

"Are you the woman I talked to last week when I was trying to get in touch with one of the Delaneys?"

Molly had thought the man's voice sounded familiar. "Yes."

"Thanks for telling me how to get hold of Dirk Delaney."

"You're quite welcome," she responded, puzzled.

"Unfortunately I didn't make any headway with him. But I got some information on Petroleum Investors. Are David and Wilson Formby still staying there?"

"Yes. David is at work. Do you want me to ring Wilson's room?"

"Please." After six rings, there was still no answer, and belatedly Molly remembered seeing Wilson leave the motel about eight, probably to keep a date. "I'm sorry. He's out." She reached for a pad and pen. "Could I take a message?"

"Just tell them Morris Abernathy called from Bangor, Maine, and ask one of them to get back to me." He gave Molly the number and rang off.

Molly stuck the message in her pocket, intending to give it to Wilson at breakfast. But the next day she put on a clean shirt and forgot about the message until midmorning, when Wilson had long since left for work. She retrieved the note during her afternoon break, intending to give it to David when he came in for dinner before his shift.

It was a wonder she hadn't forgotten more than a phone message, she told herself morosely as she tried to shake off the depression that had clung to her all day. She'd spoken to Chet briefly at breakfast, but he hadn't mentioned seeing her that evening. Nor had he mentioned her father or the accident. He had been obviously preoccupied, and she had been in the kitchen when he left for the well site. She suspected he was still trying to sort out his feelings about her and her reason for being in Sunset.

David Formby came in for dinner at five. He looked as though he hadn't been up long. "This sleeping in the daytime is for the birds," he told her. "You never feel really rested. When noises in the motel wake me up, I can't get back to sleep. Like yesterday—" He stopped abruptly as a crimson blush spread up his face.

"What about yesterday?"

He ducked his head, still blushing furiously. "Nothing. It was just somebody talking—in the hall."

Molly watched him, nonplussed. Why was he so embarrassed if that was really what he'd been about to say? Suddenly she remembered that David's room was close to hers. Yesterday afternoon Chet had stormed into her room, furious after her visit to the funeral home. "David, did you hear Chet and me arguing?"

He looked up and smiled sheepishly. "Well, a little, I guess."

How much had he heard? "I'm sorry we woke you."

"Don't worry about it. It was time to get up anyway."

Molly didn't believe him, but she let it pass. "Did you—did you hear what we were arguing about?"

He eyed her carefully, then shook his head. "Not much. It was mostly just muffled voices." He saw her dismay and added hastily, "If I had, I wouldn't spread it around."

"Oh, David, I know that." She wasn't convinced that he hadn't heard what she and Chet were saying, but David didn't strike her as the type to gossip. "I'll try to remember that you're sleeping days, and be more quiet in my room after this."

"Usually I don't hear a peep from your room. I told you, don't worry about it."

"Don't you and Wilson ever switch shifts?"

He seemed relieved to have the subject changed. "We stay on the same shift until we finish a well. It just happens to be my turn to work nights. Wilson uses sleeping pills when he's on days and can't sleep, but I don't like to resort to that." He scanned the menu halfheartedly. "I'm not very hungry. I'll have a dinner salad and a cheeseburger. And black coffee."

Molly wrote down the order. "Oh, I almost forgot." She reached in her pocket for the folded message. "Somebody called from Maine. He wants you or Wilson to phone him."

David read the message, frowning. "This Abernathy is a persistent old cuss. Wilson just wrote to him a few days ago."

It was the letter Molly had seen in the box. Had the letter prompted Abernathy to call and ask for one of the Formbys? "He said something about investing in an oil well."

"Yeah, once in a while Wilson and I have a chance to pick up an oil lease cheap. Wilson puts together a prospectus, and we sell the shares. We call our little sideline Petroleum Investors. Abernathy saw one of our ads in a Maine newspaper, and he's contacted us several times since." He grinned ruefully. "Thinks owning part of an oil well is going to make him rich."

"You'd think he'd learn," Molly said. "He mentioned that he'd bought a share in a dry hole."

David shrugged. "I don't know if it was one of ours or not."

"It must have been. He said it was a Delaney well."

"Could be. Wilson handles all that. He's a better salesman than I am."

Molly could believe it. David was too retiring to convince anyone to buy anything.

"Anyway," David went on, "Wilson wrote him and told him we'd let him know when we had some shares to sell."

"In the meantime, he called Dirk Delaney and got another turndown."

"Like I said, he's persistent. I'll have to call him back and tell him the same thing Wilson did."

When Molly went back to the kitchen to refill the water pitchers, Jude said, "I'm going to my apartment. Shouldn't be gone more than fifteen minutes."

"I thought Lauren was feeling better today."

"Oh, she is. I rented a couple of videos at the drugstore, and she probably won't move from in front of the TV set for the next three hours. But I have to get my rollaway bed and put it in Chet's room. His uncle's coming in today."

"Really? For how long?"

"Just one night. He's going back to Houston tomorrow, Chet said. I guess they have some business they have to talk over in person."

Interesting, Molly mused as she filled the last pitcher. Maybe Chet's preoccupation had nothing to do with her after all. Maybe he and his uncle had a company problem to deal with, something that had Chet worried, something too serious to be handled by phone. Whatever it was, she thought unhappily, he hadn't wanted to talk to her about it.

Dirk Delaney arrived at seven that evening. Molly saw him only at dinner when Chet introduced them. He was a tall, slender, gray-haired man with a booming voice, and he seemed to address all females as "dear." Yet he did it so innocently that you couldn't resent it. His skin was weathered to a leathery tan. He wore a Western suit with a bolo tie and cowboy boots, the image of the Texas oilman.

As she was taking their orders, Dirk Delaney gazed at her alertly, then shifted his gaze to Chet as though to confirm something to himself. Surely Chet hadn't told him that she was George Backus's daughter. No, more likely Dirk Delaney had merely picked up on the tension between her and his nephew.

The next morning, as Molly was going in for breakfast, Chet was leaving the motel by way of the lobby. When he saw her, he did an about-face and met her in the hall.

"Good morning," she said a bit stiffly.

"You're angry," he observed with a rueful quirk of one eyebrow.

She looked at him, her eyes direct, her mouth un-smiling. "No." A feeling of helplessness swamped her. How was she ever going to fall out of love with him?

She was tense, her eyes wary. She looked so vulnerable, and it was his fault. He didn't know why he should feel responsible, when she'd been deceiving him since day one, but he did. "Then your feelings are hurt."

With fingers that weren't completely steady, she pushed her hair back from her face. "I shouldn't be so touchy," she said with a shrug.

"As you know, I've had a lot on my mind."

Molly gave him a long, deliberating look. She fingered the top button of her dress. "Haven't we all?"

He closed his hand over her restless fingers and squeezed gently. "I'm not used to living in a state of mental confusion," he muttered.

She met his look, and something vibrated between them. Molly sucked in her breath. "If you're looking for sympathy, I'm fresh out."

He smiled, but his eyes remained wary. "You don't give an inch, do you?"

A hint of a frown touched her brow. "Not when I'm hanging on for dear life."

He studied her solemnly and lifted his hand to touch her hair. "Uncle Dirk's waiting in the car for me. He's leaving this evening. If it's not too late, can I see you afterward? We're going to have to talk this thing out."

After a moment, her face relaxed into a smile. "I'll check my date book."

A hint of an answering grin played across his mouth. He cupped her face in both hands, then kissed her. "You do that."

Flushed, her pulse speeding, Molly watched him leave the motel, whistling.

At nine-thirty that night Molly had showered and dressed and was propped up against her bed's headboard with her suspense novel open on her bent knees, reading to pass the time until Chet came. He hadn't returned to the motel since leaving that morning. When she took Wilson's dinner order, he said Chet and Dirk had remained at the well site. They still hadn't come in for dinner when the restaurant had closed.

Frowning, Molly closed the book. She was never going to find out who the murderer was, she thought. Every time she tried to read, distracting thoughts intruded.

At ten she was roaming the tiny room and growing angry. Where *was* Chet? Did he think all she had to do was sit in this room and wait for him to show up? Did he think she would wait forever? Well, she wouldn't!

The wind had picked up after sundown, and now it made moaning sounds at her window. It should have cooled the temperature down by now. Making a sudden decision, she went to the closet and took out her running shoes. She wasn't going to be waiting here, waiting patiently like a faithful dog, when Chet finally deigned to honor her with his presence.

She put on the shoes, grabbed her keys and left the motel by the side door. Walking across the lighted motel parking lot, the wind pushing at her back, she scanned the cars. Chet's wasn't there. Nor was his uncle's; at least, there was no car with Harris County plates. But surely Dirk had left by now. It was a good drive even to the next town large enough to have a decent motel.

Maybe Chet had had car trouble. But he could have called her to tell her that he'd be late, couldn't he?

Soon she reached a residential neighborhood and turned a corner into the wind, which carried the dry scent of dirt. It made her sneeze.

Since there were no sidewalks, she moved off the grass to the street and increased her pace to a slow jog. She hadn't jogged since leaving Dallas, and the wind resisted her forward movement. She was soon breathing hard and perspiring, but she didn't care. She needed to run off her anger and disappointment.

The street was wide, and she kept to the edge, facing oncoming traffic. Her shirt was white, and her shoes had reflecting strips across the back, so she didn't worry about the few cars that drove slowly by on the opposite side of the street, traveling in the same direction as she.

She'd let herself get out of shape, and it was hard to keep going, even at a slow jog, especially while sneezing the dust out of her nostrils every few steps. The dirt smell had grown stronger. She wondered if Sunset was in for a full-fledged dust storm. If so, it wouldn't arrive for a while yet, she told herself and ran on.

For the first two blocks she fought against slowing to a comfortable walk. Midway down the third block, she fought the urge to give up altogether and go back to the motel. When she skipped exercising strenuously for more than a few days, it was an enormous struggle to get back into it again. She kept pushing down the desire to quit and forced herself to keep going. One more block, she told herself, and then one more.

She made herself think of something besides the lifting of one foot and then the other, and the dust in her nostrils and the effort to take in more air.

Maybe she should go back to Dallas, she pondered. She hadn't learned what she'd come to Sunset for, and she was beginning to doubt that she ever would. In any case, it wouldn't bring her father back.

Dust stung her eyes. She'd better turn back soon. She wanted to be inside if a storm hit. She would run to the end of the block and then turn back.

For an instant she was dimly aware of the sound of a car approaching from behind on the opposite side of the street, but she shut it out, along with the thoughts of an approaching storm, and concentrated on reaching the next corner. Then she could turn back. She would be in her room in fifteen minutes.

She wondered if Chet had come and found her gone. Maybe he'd had second thoughts about seeing her tonight. How did he really feel about her? She didn't have long to find out. She would be returning to Dallas soon.

Leaving Sunset would mean leaving Chet, but perhaps that would be for the best. Unrequited love was too painful. It was for people who had a martyr complex, and she'd never been the type. If she hadn't come to Sunset, hadn't met Chet . . .

All at once she realized that the speed of the car coming up from behind had increased. She moved closer to the curb on her side and glanced over her shoulder. Bright headlights blinded her. She had only an instant to realize that the car was too far over on her side of the street before the driver suddenly gunned the motor and swerved toward her.

Shock paralyzed her for an instant, but the next instant she was leaping for the curb. Her quick action probably saved her life, but it wasn't quite quick enough. The car sideswiped her and knocked her down before it sped away.

She lay sprawled on her face across the curb, stunned and disoriented, listening to her own labored breathing and the whine of the wind. Dust storm coming. Her mind didn't seem to be as shaken up as her body. But how had she ended up splayed across the sidewalk like this?

After a moment she pushed herself up with her hands. Pain shot down her side, and she crumpled on her face again with a groan.

The pain seemed to clear her head. There had been bright headlights, a motor racing. Had the driver actually tried to run her down? The fearful leap of her heart made her wonder if she was in shock. The driver had probably fallen asleep at the wheel. Or maybe she hadn't been as close to the curb as she'd thought, and he simply hadn't seen her.

Gingerly, she tried to sit up. If she pushed with her left arm, the pain in her right side wasn't so severe. Struggling to a sitting position, she saw the headlights of a car coming from the same direction as the one that had hit her. Was he coming back to finish the job? In a panic, she tried to scrabble to her feet.

The car came to a screeching stop, and the driver catapulted out of it. "Molly!"

"Chet?"

"Are you all right? Oh my God!"

As she huddled on the grass, the reality of what had happened to her overwhelmed her, and she started to cry.

Then Chet was kneeling beside her, his arms enfolding her. "Oh, Molly, honey, what's wrong? Did you fall?"

She clung to him, but cried out in pain as his arms tightened around her. "My side," she gasped. "Don't touch me there...please."

He released her instantly and used his thumb to gently wipe the tears from her cheeks. He peered at her worriedly. "Tell me what happened."

"A car...it came from behind and—" She stopped to gulp down a sob. "It knocked me down."

"What! Somebody hit you? Has he gone to call an ambulance?"

She shook her head. "He didn't stop. I guess he didn't see me."

He swore savagely and then began gently moving her arms and legs. "Nothing seems to be broken." Carefully he ran a hand down her left side and then her right. She drew in a sharp breath. "It's your ribs," he muttered. "I'm going to carry you to the car. I'll try not to hurt you."

Molly nodded and bit her lip as he picked her up.

"The nearest hospital is in Snyder, and in ten minutes, when the rest of this dust hits, visibility will be nil. We won't be able to make any time. Can you stand a fifty-mile drive under those conditions?"

"I don't need to go to the hospital," she insisted. "I think I'm only bruised. Just take me back to the motel."

Reaching up to turn on the dome light, he studied her for a long moment. Her face looked very pale. "Are you sure?"

"Yes."

He started the engine and headed back to the motel. Over her protests, he insisted on carrying her to her room through wind so full of dust that it stung her face and bare arms and legs.

In her room, he laid her gently on the bed and phoned Jude's apartment. "Molly's had an accident," he said. "Can you get a doctor to come out here and examine her? He can't make it ahead of the storm now, but he should be able to start in half an hour."

"I don't need a doctor," Molly protested feebly.

He raised a hand to shush her and listened to Jude. "No, I don't think she's seriously hurt, but I want to hear a doctor say it.... You don't need to do that. Tomorrow morning will be soon enough.... Good. I'll be here to let him in." He replaced the receiver and looked at Molly. "She was in bed. She wanted to get dressed and come in here, but I put her off. You don't need three or four people crowded into this cubbyhole, hovering over you. She's calling her family doctor."

Molly was starting to feel sleepy. "Thanks," she murmured, closing her eyes.

Chet sat down on the bed and smoothed her hair away from her face. "Don't go to sleep until the doctor comes."

She turned her face to press her cheek into his palm. "You can wake me."

"Molly." He shook her gently. "You may have a concussion. You can't go to sleep yet."

She opened her eyes reluctantly. "Talk to me, then."

He stroked her hair, frowning. "Did you see the driver?"

"No."

"What about the car?"

She shook her head. "I was blinded by the headlights, and then I was trying to get out of the street."

"Didn't you hear the car coming?"

"Yes, and I moved over next to the curb. The car was on the other side of the street, and there was plenty of room. Several other cars had already passed me."

He lifted her hand to brush the knuckles with his lips. He continued to watch her gravely. "Did you get tired of waiting for me?"

She smiled dolefully. "The walls were starting to close in on me."

"I'm sorry." He turned her hand over and kissed the palm. "Uncle Dirk and I stayed late at the site. Then he wanted to find a bar and have a sandwich before he started back. I should have called you, but I kept thinking he'd leave any minute."

"Why didn't he stay another night?"

He shook his head. "I suggested that, but he said he had to be back in Houston tomorrow, and he wanted to drive part of the way tonight. Right now I'd guess he's pulled off on the shoulder to wait the storm out." He rubbed his thumb over her knuckles. "It was all very strange. I kept wondering why he'd driven all that way for only one night. When he phoned to say he was coming, I got the impression he wanted to talk about something important, in addition to visiting the well site."

"But he didn't?"

"Oh, yes." He chuckled softly. "He finally got around to it after our sandwiches. He's seeing a woman."

Molly grinned. "He had to come all this way to tell you that? Why?"

"Beats me. He's had relationships with a number of women since his divorce fourteen years ago. But this one's more important than any of the others. I gleaned that much from what he said. He always swore he'd never marry again, but I honestly think he may be considering it this time."

"Maybe he wanted you to talk him out of it," Molly murmured.

"No, it wasn't that. Nobody talks Uncle Dirk out of anything when he gets his mind set." He looked perplexed. "This one is the woman of his dreams. He actually said that. I had the feeling there was something else he wanted to say, too, but he just kept rambling on about this Suzanne." The perplexed look became a grin. "The old man's head over heels in love."

Molly ran a fingertip over the back of his hand. "I think that's sweet."

He arched a brow. "Do you?"

"Uh-huh. Everyone needs somebody to love."

"Yeah," he replied gravely.

She sensed his instinctive need to withdraw and looked away from him for a moment. She hadn't consciously meant her remark to apply to their situation, but she would have to be more careful.

"Chet," she said finally, "tonight, when I heard that car pick up speed and turned to look, I thought—" She frowned and gave a little shake of her head. "It's not all that clear in my memory now, but I do remember thinking that the driver deliberately swerved toward me." She gazed at him with worried eyes. "But that's silly, isn't it? Who would want to run over me?"

"It was an accident, honey." He looked very grim when he said it. "Try not to think about it, okay?" He kept her talking for the next half hour. The wind had abated, and the worst of the dust passed on to the south, when there was a knock at the door. "The doctor," he said, getting up.

Dr. Bocha was elderly but seemed alert and competent. "Confounded dirt," the doctor grumbled, brushing at his clothes as he entered. "We're supposed to have rain next. I'll believe that when I see it." He listened to Molly's chest, shone a light in her eyes and probed her right rib cage. She grimaced and chewed her bottom lip to keep from crying out. Then he banded wide strips of adhesive tape over her right rib cage.

"She'll be all right," he said, stuffing his stethoscope and the tape back in his bag. "The ribs aren't broken, but bruising can be almost as painful. The tape should help." He snapped his bag shut. "She might have a very mild concussion, but nothing to be concerned about. I'd recommend twenty-four hours of bed rest."

"Twenty-four hours!" Molly protested. "I'll go crazy."

The doctor looked down at her over his eyeglasses and pursed his lips. "Those ribs are going to be sorer tomorrow than they are now, young woman. You won't feel like running any races. And when you do feel up to it, I suggest that hereafter you get your exercise before dark."

Feeling reprimanded, Molly nodded wordlessly. Chet thanked the doctor for coming, paid him and saw him out. "Now," he said, turning back to Molly, "let's get you ready for bed."

He helped her out of her shorts, shirt and bra, and into a silk nightgown. She felt ridiculously embarrassed as his eyes grazed her naked body. It wasn't the first time he'd seen her without her clothes, but this was different somehow. While she pulled the nightgown down to cover her nakedness, keeping her eyes carefully averted, he drew back the bedspread and top sheet. Sighing, she settled back against the pillow and looked up at him gravely.

Chet noted that a becoming flush had replaced the pallor in her cheeks. He felt a stab of desire and was disgusted with himself for wanting her, even when she was in pain.

"Thank you for finding me," she said quietly. "And for staying until the doctor came. I'll be fine now."

He touched her hair. "I'm staying all night."

"You won't get any rest."

"I'll sleep in the chair if I need to."

"You don't have to baby-sit me. Really."

"I'm staying." He pulled the sheet up over her and smoothed it gently, as though he were tucking in a child. "I may have to go out for a little while, but I'll take your key and let myself back in. So humor me. No more arguments." He bent over to kiss her. "Now, go to sleep," he murmured before he deepened the kiss.

When he pulled away reluctantly, she smiled, her eyes still closed. "I'll come clean," she whispered drowsily. "I'm glad you're staying." The sheets felt faintly gritty from the fine dust that somehow got into the tightest places during a storm. Fortunately, she was too sleepy to be bothered by a little dust.

Chet turned out the overhead light, leaving the bathroom light on and the door slightly ajar. He sat down in the rocker and rested his head against the high back, his hands curled around the arms. Caught between the need to know more about the hit-and-run, and whether it was connected to Molly's being Backus's daughter, and the frustration of not knowing where to start, he didn't expect to get much rest.

He sat there until Molly had been asleep for some time. Then, taking her key, he let himself out quietly and drove to the police station. The officer on duty showed him into a dreary office, offered him a chair, listened to his story without comment and took a few notes.

When Chet had finished, the officer leaned back in a creaking swivel chair and eyed him doubtfully. "You say she can't describe the driver or the car?"

"The headlights blinded her."

"It was probably some kid joyriding in his dad's car."

"That doesn't excuse him."

The officer sat forward and picked up his discarded pencil, tapped it on the desk top. "Nobody said it did, Mr. Delaney. But without a description, I don't see that we can do much."

Chet hesitated before he said, "Molly—Miss Sinclair—had the distinct impression the driver meant to hit her."

The pencil tapping stopped, and the officer lifted a brow. "Why?" His tone was dry. "I mean, she's not mixed up with the Mafia or anything, is she?"

Chet took a firm hold on his temper. "I assume that's a rhetorical question."

The officer shrugged carelessly. "Look, Mr. Delaney. You say Miss Sinclair has been in Sunset a short time. She's a stranger to most of our citizens. Who would want to harm her?"

Chet expelled a long breath. "Maybe nobody does, but she swears that car swerved toward her as she was trying to get out of the way."

"That could be explained several ways. The driver could have fallen asleep, for one. It's still a hit-and-run, of course, and that's against the law. But about the only thing I can do is question the people who live in that block and see if anyone saw the car."

Chet had little doubt that the officer would keep his word, but it might be a halfhearted attempt, since Molly hadn't been seriously hurt. If the Sunset police department was like most small-town forces, it was undermanned, which meant a nonfatal hit-and-run with no witnesses would necessarily rank low on their priority list. He knew of only one thing that might cause them to investigate more thoroughly.

"There's something else you should know, but for Molly's sake, I wouldn't want it to get out. She's the daughter of George Backus, the man who was killed when his car went into the lake."

A puzzled alertness flashed in the officer's eyes. "The Driving under the Influence last April?"

"Yes, only she's convinced he wasn't drunk. He'd been a recovering alcoholic for fifteen years. She came to Sunset with some notion of gathering evidence to support her belief. As far as I know, nobody but me knows that she has any connection to Backus.''

"You're saying this Sinclair woman *might* be right? And somebody else *might* know who she is? And that somebody *might* have been involved in Backus's death? That's a lot of mights, Mr. Delaney."

Chet frowned. "I know. Before this hit-and-run, I was convinced she was on a wild-goose chase. Now, I'm not quite so sure. Did anybody check Backus's car when it was pulled from the lake to see if it had been tampered with?''

The officer stiffened defensively. "We had no reason to. There were witnesses who said he was drunk. It was an open-and-shut case. The judge ruled it an accidental death. And the car's scrap metal in some salvage yard by now."

Chet decided he'd pressed as hard as he prudently could. "But you will check with the people who live in the block where Molly was hit?"

"I said I would. If I get any leads, I'll follow up on them." His tone said he didn't expect to get any.

Chet rose. "Thank you. I'm sure Molly will feel better knowing something's being done."

When Chet got back to the motel, Molly was still asleep. He closed the door quietly and dropped into the rocking chair. He felt as though the trip to the police station had been futile. But at least he'd covered every base he could think of. A part of him still felt the odds were in favor of the hit-and-run being an accident. Another part wondered what the odds were for both members of the Backus family being involved in car accidents while in Sunset.

He couldn't sleep. He continued his vigil there as the minutes and hours ticked away, watching Molly sleep, and kept awake himself with a parade of disturbing thoughts.

Chapter 10

Every half hour or so, Chet checked on Molly, laying a hand on her forehead to see if she felt feverish and assuring himself that she was breathing normally. Finally he abandoned the chair altogether to stand and stare out the window at the lighted parking lot.

What in God's name is going on here? he wondered, passing a frustrated hand over his face. He'd had a moment of pure panic when he'd found Molly lying half in the street, obviously hurt. The mere memory could still cause a band of fear to tighten around his heart.

He kneaded the taut muscles at the back of his neck. Had the driver of that car tonight really tried to run Molly down? The police didn't believe it, and he didn't want to believe it, either. Letting out a long breath, he began to sift the question around in his mind, looking at it from different angles.

At the very least, he pondered grimly, it had been an accidental hit-and-run, as the police believed, which could mean that the driver had been drunk or, at any rate, speeding. A reckless teenager, maybe. It was for damn sure he was a cowardly SOB. If Chet ever learned the driver's identity, he wasn't sure he could keep himself from hurting him. His hands clenched at his sides. If Molly had been seriously hurt . . . if he hadn't found her so quickly . . .

He jerked his mind back on track. At worst, the hit-and-run had been a deliberate attempt at murder. It was the first time he'd actually let the word penetrate his conscious mind. Now it lay there like a ticking bomb, except that a bomb would be easier to deal with. He could pitch it out the window and cover Molly's body with his own to protect her from the blast.

If someone was trying to kill Molly, he couldn't depend on the police to protect her. Nor could he fully protect her himself if he didn't know who and why. And when they might try again. His skin prickling with nervous tension, he stepped into the bathroom and closed the door. He splashed cold water on his face and stared at himself in the mirror.

Before tonight, he had more or less dismissed Molly's claim that her father's death hadn't been an accident. It was too preposterous to think that a man like George Backus could have any violent enemies. He had told himself that refusing to accept the death as a simple accident was Molly's way of dealing with her grief.

He reached for a towel and dried his face. Backus's letter had continued to trouble him, though. Backus's saying that Chet and his uncle were up to something didn't make sense. Up to what, for God's sake? He'd finally decided that it had just been the alcohol talking.

Chet returned the towel to its rack, eased the bathroom door open and checked on Molly again. She hadn't moved since the last time he'd looked. Grateful that she was able to rest, he studied her profile—the slightly open mouth, the curve of her cheek, the cloud of black hair against the pillow. She was so lovely and so vulnerable. Watching her sleep, thinking about her, made him feel restless. It wasn't simply that he wanted her. After all, he'd known that feeling with other women.

He swallowed a sudden thickness in his throat. Good God, he thought, still staring at her. Was he in love with her? No, that was, well, unacceptable. A man didn't go through life carefully structuring his relationships with women, always testing the waters, knowing when things were about to get sticky in time to back off, and then suddenly fall in love without knowing when it happened. Besides, how could he be so sure it was love if he'd never been in love before?

Swell, Delaney, he thought angrily as he stepped back and braced himself with both hands gripping the bed's footboard. He remembered Dirk sitting in that bar tonight and running on about this new woman of his. Dirk, the confirmed misogynist, had suddenly done an about-face. At the age of sixty, he was in love and, though he hadn't said it in so many words, planning to propose to his Suzanne. Once, Chet would have bet anything he had that such a thing would never happen.

Obviously he didn't know his uncle as well as he'd always thought. Why, for instance, had Dirk felt it necessary to deliver the news in person? Chet still had a feeling of waiting for the other shoe to fall.

It brought to mind other questions he'd asked himself about his uncle lately. For one thing, he wondered how his uncle had come up with the cash to drill the previous well—the one Backus had worked on—so quickly. When Chet had asked, Dirk had evaded the question. Had Dirk indulged in a bit of overly creative financing that wouldn't stand up to close scrutiny? Could Backus have been referring to that when he said the Delaneys were up to something? But even if Dirk had stepped over the line of good financial sense, how could Backus have discovered it?

Deeply troubled, Chet stretched and massaged the back of his neck again. Last night he'd told his uncle who Molly really was and about the letter her father had written to her. He'd wanted to talk it over with someone, and Dirk had seemed safe, since he was leaving the next day and couldn't let it slip. Dirk had been amazed by Backus's vague accusation, had said he had no idea what the man could have meant.

Then Dirk had started talking about Suzanne, keeping Chet in the bar until after ten. Chet had urged him to spend another night in Sunset, but Dirk had left him on the sidewalk after making a phone call from the bar, driving down Main Street toward the highway. Chet had gone back to the motel, to Molly's room. Upon discovering she wasn't there, he'd realized that she'd grown tired of waiting for him and had probably gone out for a walk. He'd found her only minutes after she'd been hit, no more than twenty minutes since he'd watched his uncle's car driving down the street away from him. Heading out of town, he'd assumed.

Appalled at the direction his thoughts were taking, Chet swore quietly. Was he losing his mind? Dirk couldn't have known that Molly was on that street. Unless—unless that phone call Dirk had made before leaving the bar had been to Molly instead of Suzanne, as he'd assumed. If Dirk had phoned her room and gotten no answer, it wouldn't have been difficult to chance upon her if he'd been driving around, trying to decide what to do.

Impossible, Chet told himself savagely. Dirk *had* left town. His uncle was a tough old bird, but he wasn't a murderer.

Still, Chet could no longer tell himself that the hit-and-run had been an accident. Nor could he continue to believe, without serious doubts, that Molly was on a wild-goose chase, just trying to keep from accepting her father's death for what it was.

Molly stirred and mumbled something. She turned her head and peered up at him. "Chet?"

He moved to the side of the bed. "Yeah, I'm here. Do you feel okay?"

"Uh-huh," she murmured sleepily. "Just sore."

He pulled the sheet up over her shoulders. "Go back to sleep, honey."

"You can't stay up all night. Why don't you get in bed with me and try to sleep?"

"There isn't room. Besides, I'd be afraid of hurting you."

"I'll let you know if you hurt me." She slowly shifted over in the narrow bed. "See, there's plenty of room."

Chet was weary and sick of his own thoughts. He wasn't going to solve anything tonight by thinking about it any longer. All he was going to do was get more confused. She looked so warm and inviting, curled on her side beneath the sheet.

Hesitating no longer, he undressed down to his briefs and carefully slid in beside her, curling his chest and legs to fit the contours of her body. She snuggled back against him. "That's much better," she murmured, already drifting back to sleep. "Try not to touch my side."

Chet rested a hand lightly on her thigh. "Is that all right?"

"Wonderful," she sighed, and the next thing he knew she was asleep, breathing slowly and quietly.

"Molly," he murmured as she sighed in sleep.

When she didn't respond, he kissed the curve of her shoulder and her hair, then settled against her as comfortably as he could and tried to ignore the hunger that had flared up when he curled his body against hers.

She felt so soft and warm.

It felt so right to have her sleeping this way, curled back against him. Slowly his desire was replaced by an aching tenderness. He began to relax and feel sleepy, already anticipating waking beside her.

Sunlight streaming through the open slats of the window blind heated his face, waking him. He started to turn over and stretch, then felt Molly's warm thigh beneath his hand and got out of bed as quietly as possible. But she woke up anyway.

Turning on her back, she closed her eyes against the sunlight and smiled. "Did you sleep?"

He was tugging on his trousers. "Uh-huh."

"So did I. Like a log." She struggled to sit up in bed, grimaced as she plumped the pillow behind her, then sank back with a sigh. "Yuck, I feel grungy. I need a hot shower."

"You're not supposed to get up."

"I'll feel worse lying here. These sheets need washing as badly as I do. And hot water might take away some of my soreness. Besides, I can't leave Jude to wait on all those tables by herself."

"Okay, Molly, you can stop **ratio**nalizing. I give up. But," he said warningly, "you're not leaving this room. You can take a shower if you feel up to it, but I'm going to tell Jude you can't work today." He buttoned his shirt and sat in the rocker to put on his socks and shoes. "I'll bring your breakfast in later."

She sighed heavily. "Okay, I'll stay here until after noon. But if I'm feeling better, I'm going to work the dinner shift at least the busiest part of it."

He stood beside the bed, looking down at her with a determined expression. "We'll see."

She said nothing as he bent to kiss her, then left with a final word of caution. "Don't open this door to anybody but me or Jude."

By the time he returned with her breakfast on a tray, she'd showered and dressed with careful movements punctuated by groans of frustration. But she had no intention of telling Chet how hard it had been to fasten her bra and get her arms into the sleeves of her blouse. When he'd said, "Molly, let me in," she had opened the door, a serene smile on her face.

She sat in the rocker, the tray across her lap. Chet helped himself to the second mug of coffee on the tray and settled on the side of the bed, which Molly had managed to strip of its sheets. Discovering that she was ravenous, she attacked the food with gusto.

Watching her over his mug, Chet said, "I want you to promise me not to go out alone at night again, Molly."

She looked up at him seriously. "After what happened last night, that'll be an easy promise to keep."

"I went to the police and reported the hit-and-run."

She stared at him in surprise. "When?"

"Last night, while you were asleep."

She chewed on her bottom lip. "I guess I'm glad. Actually, I've been thinking about doing it myself."

"I had to tell them that George was your father and why you're in Sunset."

She looked alarmed. "Chet—"

"I'm sure they'll be discreet. I said we didn't want anyone else to know. I have to tell you, though, that I didn't get the impression they're interested in investigating your father's death at this point. Whatever evidence there might have been is no longer available to them."

"Since I didn't see the car that hit me, they don't have much to go on there, either."

"They'll question people who live on the block where you were hit, in case anyone saw the car."

She sighed. "That's something." She picked up her fork and began to eat.

"Tell me again everything you remember about what happened, starting from when you left the motel."

She laid down her fork to lift her coffee mug in both hands. "I waited for you until ten and then—" She cocked her head as he lifted a brow. "I thought you'd stood me up, and I was mad. In case you did decide to show up so late, I didn't want you to find me here, waiting like a—a pathetic wimp.''

He gave a burst of appreciative laughter. "A wimp you're not, Molly." As her troubled eyes cleared and she smiled at him, he was swept with a wave of emotion—warm joy at merely being with her and cold fear for her safety. "So you went for a walk to teach me a lesson."

She sobered and took a thoughtful sip of her coffee. "Yeah, only I was the one who learned a lesson." She set her mug down and picked up a piece of toast to spread jelly on it.

"I wanted to run," she went on, "so I had to get into the street. I haven't jogged since I left Dallas, and I've gotten soft. I was sucking in air—and dust—like a beached whale." She took a bite of toast. "I hate it when I let myself get out of shape and have to go through all the agony again. You know how it is. I was playing those little mind games with myself, telling myself I could stop and walk when I reached the end of the block, and when I got there, that I had to go one more block. And then just one more."

He waited patiently, letting her work her way up to the hit-and-run in her own time. "Your mind was on your body, not on things outside it."

She nodded, lifting the toast for another bite. "I didn't meet any cars traveling toward me. I was vaguely aware when a car passed me on the other side of the street. There were three of them before the one that hit me."

She bit into the toast again and frowned as she chewed. "I heard it behind me. I'm sure I moved over close to the curb. I was struggling to keep on running, and all at once I heard the motor speed up. I looked over my shoulder and—'' She put down the toast and gave him a long, troubled look. ''I swear, Chet, that car came right at me. If I hadn't jumped away, it would have gone over me instead of sideswiping me. It's possible the driver simply lost control and, when he realized he'd hit me, was too scared to stop.''

He could see she wanted to believe that and schooled his voice to remain noncommittal. ''That could be what happened. It probably is. But you can't take any more chances. Have you thought about going back to Dallas?''

''You mean now?''

He nodded gravely. ''If somebody is trying to scare you off, you should be safe back there.'' He believed the driver had meant to do far worse than scare her, but there was no point in frightening her any more than was necessary to make her cautious.

Did he want her to leave solely for her own good, Molly wondered, or was his own peace of mind a factor? She knew that she disturbed him, even if he wasn't in love with her. ''If somebody's trying to scare me off, it means they know why I'm here.''

After a moment's hesitation, he nodded. With the coming of day, he'd realized how ridiculous his nighttime suspicions of his uncle were. If Molly was in danger, it wasn't from Dirk. ''You didn't tell anyone else, did you?''

She looked unhappy. ''No, but David Formby may know. He heard us arguing after you'd been to the funeral home. I don't know how much he understood, but—'' she lifted her shoulders —''maybe enough. He let it slip that we'd awakened him. When I asked what he'd heard, he said 'nothing but muffled voices.' ''

But David, out of embarrassment, if nothing else, wouldn't admit he'd heard their argument, Chet thought. And he certainly wouldn't admit it if he'd felt threatened by what he'd heard. "Remember that phone call from the guy who wanted to invest in a Delaney well?" He'd been about to make a point, but it eluded him—a strange thought that flickered at the back of his mind for an instant, but now it was gone.

"Yes. His name's Abernathy. He lives in Maine. He called again the night before last. He'd talked to your uncle about investing in a well, but apparently he was turned down. When he called back, he asked to speak to Wilson or David."

"Didn't he tell you the first time that he'd once owned a share of a Delaney well?"

Molly nodded. "A dry hole, he said. Anyway, I meant to give the message to Wilson at breakfast the next morning, but I forgot it. So I gave it to David that afternoon." For a moment they just looked at each other, absorbed in their own thoughts. Then Molly added, "Oh, and you were right about David and Wilson having a second business on the side. David said they occasionally pick up an oil lease and sell shares. Abernathy connected with them through an ad in a Maine newspaper. He keeps pestering them to get in on another well. David said Abernathy thinks he's going to get rich investing in oil."

"So," Chet said, thinking aloud, "if Uncle Dirk gave the Formbys a chunk of the first well in the Sunset field in lieu of salary, they could have sold a piece of it to this Abernathy."

"I asked David about that. He said he didn't know. Wilson does the selling, he said." She frowned suddenly. "Now that I think about it, though, it seems odd that David wouldn't know what's going on. Wouldn't they talk about it?"

He rose restlessly, still holding his mug. "It's hard to believe they don't. David might leave the selling up to Wilson, but he's no fool. He must keep up with what's going on." He drank the last of his coffee and set the empty mug down, his mind still working at the hopeless tangle of questions. "We had so many other things to talk about, I forgot to ask Uncle Dirk if he'd signed over any shares in that last well to the Formbys." He thrust his hands into his pockets and gazed out the window. "He should be back in Houston by tonight, tomorrow at the latest. I'll call and ask him then."

Molly set her tray on the floor and pushed herself up. Chet had his back to her. "What are you thinking?"

He turned around, his eyes perplexed. "Nothing. I'm at a total loss."

"You don't think this Abernathy has some connection to what's been happening to me?"

He went to her and placed his hands on her shoulders. "No, honey. I'm floundering. None of this makes any sense."

She looked up at him with frightened eyes. "Were you able to find out anything from your uncle that throws any light on what Dad said in his letter?"

"No." He bent to kiss the top of her head, afraid to hold her as he really wanted to for fear of hurting her. Molly didn't trust Dirk, he realized. Not that she had any reason to, since she didn't know him. It had probably already occurred to her that Dirk could still have been in Sunset when she was hit by that car. It was only natural that the coincidence would seem suspicious to her. He almost wished he hadn't told Dirk about that letter.

She dropped her head and rested her forehead on his chest for a moment. He touched his chin to the top of her head and stroked her hair. "I have the records on that first well out at the site. I'll look up the land-owner who granted us the lease and contact him. Maybe he sold his sixteenth share to Abernathy."

She looked up at him. "But Abernathy said he bought it through Petroleum Investors. That's the Formbys' company."

"Yeah," Chet agreed with a heavy sigh, "but we've got to find a loose thread somewhere in this tangle and start pulling on it, or we're never going to get to the bottom of the mess."

"I guess so."

Chet leaned over and nuzzled her ear. "I know I can't keep you from working the dinner shift if you're determined," he whispered, "but don't leave the motel at night unless I'm with you."

"I won't," she murmured, turning her head so that her lips met his.

He lingered over her mouth for several moments, then drew away with a reluctant groan. "Kissing you only makes me want to do other things."

"Oh." Molly gave him an understanding smile. "I know." She relaxed against him for an instant. "My ribs won't be sore forever."

"True." He grinned at her. "Right now, I have things to do and phone calls to make." He kissed her nose. "I'll be back to check on you later."

"You're pampering me," she murmured.

"Yeah, and I'm starting to like it."

She laughed. "You don't have to look so worried about it."

He raised her hand to his lips. "Maybe I do."

Chapter 11

It was night, and Molly was out on the street again, running. She must have run a long way, because she didn't recognize any of the houses. As she ran on, the street became narrower and the houses fewer. She was in the country. She had to turn back.

She reversed her direction, realizing that she was lost. How strange. How could anyone get lost in Sunset? But maybe this wasn't Sunset.

Frightened, she ran faster, turned a corner and saw the headlights of a car coming toward her very fast. Her heart racing in terror, she darted to one side and ran headlong into a wire fence that stretched along the edge of the street. There was no curb, no shoulder, only the fence and the street, with no space in between.

The car was nearly upon her. She could see the driver, a gray-haired man. He was bent over the steering wheel, his lips curled back from his teeth in a snarl.

He meant to hit her! In a full panic, she grabbed hold of the fence with both hands and tried to pull herself up. Her foot caught on something, and she hung there, helpless. She screamed the instant before the car crashed into her.

"Molly. Molly!" Heart pounding, Chet shook her gently. "Molly, wake up, it's a dream." Clasping her shoulders, he shook her a little harder, but she kept tossing her head from side to side on the pillow and whimpering pitifully.

"It's all right, Molly. You're in bed in the motel. Molly." He took her face in his hands and felt her cool, damp skin. "It's Chet, honey," he said quietly. "I won't let anybody hurt you."

Molly felt her chest heaving for air and forced her eyes open. She was shivering. Chet's hands on her face were warm, his voice low and soothing.

The panic was receding. She made herself breathe more calmly and waited for the fear to pass.

Only a dream, she told herself. She was in bed. Chet's bed. She had stubbornly insisted on working the dinner shift for more than two hours. Then she'd made the wrong move too quickly, and pain had throbbed down her side. Jude had seen her grab the edge of a table to keep from falling.

"I knew you shouldn't be in here," Jude had said, then had gone in search of Chet.

Chet had brought her to his room, saying, "I'm going to stay with you, but I won't spend another night sharing that twin bed of yours. My bed's queen-size. I won't be rolling over on you in my sleep."

She hadn't argued. She'd had a dim impression of a room and a bed, both three times the size of hers. She barely remembered Chet helping her out of her clothes and into one of his T-shirts. He had led her to the bed, and that was the last thing she remembered. Why was she sleeping so much? Maybe she *had* suffered a mild concussion, as the doctor had suggested.

The only other time she could remember sleeping so much was the first couple of weeks after her marriage broke up. It had been a way to block out reality. It could be that she was doing the same thing now.

"I'll bring you some water."

"And aspirin."

"All right."

It was raining, she realized, finally identifying the insistent drumming sound on the roof. In her dream, the sound had been transformed into the noise of a car's motor racing. Shuddering, she pulled the sheet over her. Chet returned with water in a plastic cup and two tablets. She rose up on her left elbow to drink. "What time is it?"

"Two a.m."

"How long has it been raining?"

"Since about ten, and it doesn't seem to be slacking off any." He took the empty cup from her hand and dropped it in the wastebasket. He slipped back into the bed, turning on his side toward her. "Better?"

"Yes." He'd left the bathroom light on, and she could see the drawn lines in his face. He hadn't slept much the past two nights.

Even though he'd placed her so that the bruised side of her body wasn't next to him, he had been very careful to stay on his side of the bed during the night, never making contact with her body. Now he touched her arm lightly. "Molly, traumatic events often cause nightmares. I know I had lots of nightmares when my parents died. It helps to talk about them, though. Why don't you tell me what you were dreaming about.''

She could talk about it now. The reality of Chet and the motel room was blunting the dream's sharp edges. ''It was night. I was running.'' She lay on her back, clutching the sheet beneath her chin. ''There was a car, and I tried to climb a fence, and—'' She remembered the driver then, hunched over the wheel, murderous hatred contorting his face. It had been Dirk Delaney. She turned her head to peer at Chet in the dim light. ''—then you woke me. Did I cry out?''

''You were groaning. I'm glad I was here. You overdid it in the restaurant tonight. You weren't ready to return to work, but I guess you had to find that out for yourself.''

His hand resting lightly on her upper arm was warm and comforting, and she felt herself relaxing. Her heartbeat was steady now. ''I've never liked being told what to do,'' she admitted.

''I noticed. I expected more of an argument when I brought you here for the night.''

She smiled. ''At that point, I didn't care where you took me, just so I could lie down. But I'd have been all right on my own.''

''Yeah, well, *I* wouldn't have been. I wanted to be able to wake up and know you were safe.''

''Chet . . .'' Without realizing it, she moved closer to him. ''Have you talked to your uncle since he left Sunset?'' The image of the driver in her dream was fading, but the feeling of being caught and helpless, lingered. Even if it had been only a dream, she would feel better knowing that Dirk Delaney was back in Houston.

"No." He rolled on his back and gazed at the ceiling. "I called his place before I went to bed, but he wasn't there. I did get hold of the man who leased us the drilling rights on that last well, though. He held on to his sixteenth share. After we got a dry hole, of course, he wished he'd sold it. Hindsight is wonderful." He was silent for a moment before he added, "I'll try Uncle Dirk again tomorrow. I want some answers."

She laid her head against his shoulder and wound her arm around him. "You sound worried."

He braced himself against the flood of tenderness unleashed in him by her closeness. There was desire, too, but it was the tenderness, the need to protect her, care for her, that he wasn't ready to examine yet. He shifted to put his arm around her, settling her head against his shoulder once more. "It's just business," he said. "I'd rather not talk about it."

She sighed. "Are you sleepy?"

"No." He tried to ignore the bulge of her breast against his side and the light pressure of her small hand on his chest.

"Tell me about your childhood," she said idly. "How old were you when your parents died?"

He was silent for a moment, his right hand stroking the curve of her shoulder. Then he laid his hand over hers on his chest. "Twelve."

"I'm sorry." She turned her hand over to lace her fingers with his and squeezed gently. "I'm so sorry. I know how it must have hurt. I was only thirteen when my mother died of a heart attack. She hadn't been really well for about a year, but nobody expected her to die so suddenly.''

''Is that when your father stopped drinking?''

''Yes. He blamed himself for her death. He was sleeping off a drunk on the sofa that night. When he woke up and found her in their bed, she'd been dead for hours.''

''Where were you?''

''Away at camp. Dad sent his aunt to pick me up and break the news to me. I—I thought I'd die, too, at first. I didn't want to live. But Dad was there for me. I never saw him take another drink. It was the one good thing to come out of Mother's death.''

''The only positive thing about losing my parents was that I didn't have to listen to them fight anymore.'' The hand on her shoulder stilled, and she could feel him tense. ''I've always thought they were arguing in the car that night. Dad must've taken his eyes off the road. He hit a concrete bridge support. The police said the car had been traveling at sixty-five miles an hour.''

They were both silent for a moment, imagining the impact, the crushing of metal and glass and two lives. ''My parents never fought. Sometimes...'' She trailed off, wondering if she'd gotten in too deep, introducing the subject of their childhoods. She'd come to terms with hers, but Chet's tenseness made her wonder if he had.

''What?''

''I think it's better to fight than to suffer in silence. If Mother had stood up to Dad about his drinking, he might have quit sooner.''

"It may be better for the two people involved, but if there are children..."

"Maybe you're right." She turned her face into the hollow of his neck, instinctively seeking comfort. "From what you've said, I guess you just exchanged one battleground for another when you moved in with Dirk."

He uttered a soft, ironic laugh. "There were times when I wondered if I'd dreamed my parents were dead. I'd wake up at night and hear Dirk and Charlotte going at it, and for an instant I'd think I was back in my folks' house."

"That must have been horrible," she murmured. "You were only a child."

He shrugged. "I grew up fast. I learned to block it out, but I was damn glad when I could go away to college. That's when Charlotte decided to leave, too. I guess she'd stayed in the marriage that long out of some sense of obligation to me. No one should have to do that."

"I know. It's better for kids to grow up with a single parent than with two parents who make each other miserable. Some people are simply wrong for each other."

"If only they would make a clean break before there are any children. Marriage and children just don't work for certain people."

"It's hard for them to admit they've made a mistake," she mused. "After all, they were once in love and thought they could be happy together. So they hang in there, hoping things will go back to the way they were."

"Is that what you did?"

"Well, I…" She tilted her head back and looked into his eyes for a long moment. "I guess so. Things didn't get really bad until Tom lost his job ten months after we were married." She turned her head on his shoulder, averting her gaze. "I was working, and we were able to get by until he found something else, so I didn't think it was any big deal."

"But he did," he observed.

"He seemed to resent the fact that I was working and he wasn't. Eventually I realized that had nothing to do with it. He'd decided he didn't want to be married, and he used being out of a job to justify his rotten moods. Being married bored Tom. I suppose he expected it to be the way it was when we were dating, all fun and parties. After we split up, he partied for two years until he married again. She was nineteen. It lasted about six months."

"Did it…?" He hesitated, wondering what business her marriage and divorce were of his. Why did it matter? "Did it bother you when he married again?"

"You mean was I jealous? No. By then I felt lucky to be out of it. I loved him in a naive sort of way when we got married, but I was too young to know that love that lasts only as long as things are going well isn't deep enough to build a marriage on."

"Do you ever see him?"

"The last time was… let me see… more than three years ago. Last I heard, he'd moved to San Francisco. I wish him well, but I can't imagine what we'd talk about if we met now."

He toyed idly with the ribbed neck of the T-shirt she wore. Sighing, she snuggled against him contentedly. He went still for an instant, then shifted uncomfortably, removing his arm from around her shoulders. He lay with both arms at his sides. "We'd better stop talking," he muttered, "so you can sleep."

She ignored his withdrawal and moved her hand back to his bare chest. "I'm not sleepy." She slid her palm slowly down until it rested just below his rib cage. "I love to touch you."

"Molly—"

She rose up on her elbow until her mouth could skim over his shoulder and chest, tasting his flesh. She nibbled at a taut male nipple, then rubbed her cheek against his hair-roughened chest, listening to the thunder of his heart. She felt him tremble and lie very still. "What were you saying, Chet?"

"Don't do this to me."

She let her hand roam. "What am I doing to you?"

"Driving me crazy. If you don't stop, you'll force me to spend the rest of the night on the floor. I'll have no other choice."

"Oh, I wouldn't say that." She slid her fingers beneath the waistband of his briefs. "You could stay here and make love to me."

He removed her hand from his briefs and placed it carefully on the curve of her hip, as though he were moving a live grenade out of harm's way. He raised up and pressed a hand to her shoulder until she was lying on her back, looking up at him with a soft smile. She couldn't read his thoughts in his eyes, only the desire.

"I'd hurt you," he said.

"No, you wouldn't. I'm much better." Taking his hand, she placed it on her breast.

Need tore through him. "Oh God, Molly—"

Slowly her arms went around his neck. "Make love to me, Chet."

He found himself unable to resist. Passion blotted out everything else, including his fear of hurting her. He watched the tip of her tongue moisten her bottom lip invitingly, and then he bent to take her mouth. He took the kiss deep, but lazily, slowly, letting the passion build, layer by layer, until there was nothing else for either of them.

He still smelled of the shower he'd taken before coming to bed. It must have been very late, she thought dreamily. The scent of soap clung to his skin. She breathed it in, letting it fill her. Had he delayed coming to bed until he was too tired to be driven mad by her sleeping beside him? No matter how many emotional defenses he constructed against her, she realized that he couldn't deny his need for her. For tonight, that was enough.

In the light from the bathroom, she could see him. It pleased her to watch the ripple of the muscles in his arms as he braced himself above her, instinctively keeping his full weight from resting against her bruised rib cage. She loved watching the shifting planes and angels of his face and his eyes darkening with passion, his need open and exposed for her to see.

Beneath her hands, his shoulders were damp with perspiration. She could feel the moist sheen as she ran her palms over his skin. She watched his eyes as he kissed her hungrily, saw the glaze of passion come over them and felt a matching desire pulsing in her own body.

To each of them, the other's body was perfect as no other's had ever been. Instinctively, they knew how best to please each other. The intensity of Molly's need kept pace with his. Simultaneously, their breathing speeded up and became labored. Their hearts pounded with the same frantic rhythm. This, Molly thought dizzily, is what it means to be made for each other.

When he touched her, she trembled. Her flesh hummed with an intensity of pleasure that she had never felt with anyone else. Wonder and need merged, and neither of them held anything back. This was an intimacy more powerful and complete than they had allowed themselves to experience before.

They flowed with it, sharing the pleasure. Chet couldn't keep his emotional barriers from crumbling, and he didn't try. For the first time he accepted that he loved her, and he told her with his body, if not with words. She was the other part of him, the part that made him complete. He wanted her—body, mind and spirit—with him always. He wanted to share her happiness and her sorrow. He wanted to know what she was thinking before she said it. He wanted to believe that the intimacy didn't have to end.

The stream of light from the bathroom fell across her face. Her gray eyes were dark and dazed with passion. Her mouth was soft and yielding. Her hair was tangled black silk against the white pillow. Her damp skin gleamed golden with an inner fire. Except in dreams, he had never imagined a woman existed who would love him so naturally, so freely, a woman who could be so accepting of her own sexuality. This must be how it had been with the first man and woman, before civilization taught them to tame the wildness.

She murmured his name and smiled up at him with her face aglow. She moved with him easily, fluidly, as though she had always known him. It could never be like this with anyone else. He would remember her like this always, would keep these feelings and this moment with him for the rest of his life, even if he were separated from her by ten thousand miles.

Molly, he thought dizzily as their bodies merged. There was never anyone like you. There never will be. It was as though, for the first time in his life, he had come home.

He watched her eyes close as he took her to the edge. And then he could no longer see, and there was only staggering sensation and ecstatic release as he gave himself to her.

Chapter 12

Molly awoke to the sound of rain pelting the roof. She reached out for Chet, but her arm found only the bed. The warmth of his body lingered in the sheets. Sighing, she sat up and realized that water was running in the shower. Until she was fully awake, the sound had been lost in the noise of the pounding rain.

The sky beyond the windowpane and the deluge of water were both dark gray and gloomy. Sitting there, with her knees drawn up, Molly was reminded of summer mornings during her childhood when it had rained so hard that work in the oil fields was temporarily halted. Even now, the memories of those rare times when she and her father had been confined to their house or a motel all day long were warm and treasured. They had entertained themselves playing cards and board games; if they were at home, they had often spent the afternoon baking two or three kinds of cookies and sampling them while they were still warm, with glasses of cold milk.

Hearing the shower go off, she got out of bed and dressed. She tapped on the bathroom door, then opened it. Chet stood in his briefs, shaving in front of the foggy mirror.

He turned around. "Good morning." He turned back to the mirror and drew the razor up the underside of his tilted chin. "Did you sleep well?"

She picked up the towel he'd used and dried the places on his back that he'd missed. "Uh-huh. I half woke up sometime early this morning, but I dropped right back to sleep. Did you know you snore?"

He smiled at her reflection in the mirror. "So I've been told."

"I see." She tilted her head. "By whom?"

"Oh, no, you don't. I'm not walking into that one. Uncle Dirk told me."

She gave a quiet laugh as she tossed the towel over a rack. "Of course he did," she said sweetly.

He grinned. "The night shift hit oil last night, right after the rain started. David knocked on the door earlier to tell me."

"That's wonderful news!" Her words were sincere; she knew the drilling company needed to find oil. But it also meant that Chet would be leaving Sunset soon. They both would be. With a long sigh, she wrapped her arms around his waist and pressed her lips to his back. She sensed his resistance and let her hands fall. "Is it a big hit?"

"We don't know yet, but it looks good. We'll get the pump in as soon as this rain stops, and then we'll see."

"You'll be winding things up here, then."

"In another week or so." He clamped his lips together and shaved beneath his nose. "Are you going to work today?"

"I doubt we'll have much lunch business with this rain, but I'll pitch in if Jude needs me. I'm not nearly as sore this morning. I'll use my own bed tonight so I don't disturb your sleep."

He laid his razor on the edge of the washbasin and turned to run a hand over her tousled curls. "You disturb my sleep even when we're not in the same bed." Sighing, he folded her in his arms and rested his chin on top of her head.

She let herself relax against him and closed her eyes. "That's nice."

"That's not exactly the way I'd describe it," he murmured. He drew away until their eyes met again. "But somehow I think we need some nights apart," he said cautiously. "Things are moving too fast for me. Can you try to understand that?"

She opened her mouth to say that, with them, it couldn't have happened slowly. The feelings were too strong. But she wondered if he would understand her sureness, the absolute certainty that she would never love anyone else with the same intensity. "I know exactly what you mean," she said instead, touching her lips to his lightly. "These last few days, we've shared something very special. Let's not tempt fate by asking for more."

Fighting back the need to say he already wanted more and was terrified by the implications of that, Chet gathered her close again. "For now, we won't," he agreed, and felt an astonishing surge of gratitude at her willingness to allow whatever would be to be. "You

know, I'm going to regret leaving here, though. I've
even grown attached to that ugly orange bedspread.''

She tilted her head back and gave him a wry grin.
''Amazing what you can get used to living with when
your mind's on other things.''

''Yeah.'' He took advantage of her upturned mouth
to kiss her. She tasted shaving cream.

''Chet.'' As he nibbled at her earlobe, she took a
deep breath. ''I need to go back to my room to shower
and change clothes, so I can have breakfast. I'm
famished.''

''Sex and a good sleep do tend to make one hungry.'' He ran his lips along her jawline. ''But what's
another half hour—''

''Chet, I mean it. I'm about to start gnawing on the
woodwork.''

''That sounds serious,'' he murmured, and with reluctance released her. ''Okay. I'll try Uncle Dirk's
number again, and then I'll meet you in the restaurant. If you get there first, you can start without me.''

''Thank you so much,'' she said dryly and stepped
around him to the open bathroom doorway. The moment the contact between them had been broken, she'd
felt the beginning of tension in the pit of her stomach.
Childish, she told herself. She was a grown woman who
had learned how to survive. She was strong enough to
take what he was willing to give and to let go when he
did. She would still love him, and it would hurt like the
devil, but she would go on working and living. She
would stop hurting eventually. She would even be
happy again. Wouldn't she?

''Nobody will be able to work at the site today, even
if the rain stops soon,'' he began as she moved toward

the door. "Maybe we can get a card game going after breakfast." Why did he have this need to keep her there? To talk to her until they both felt reassured that last night had made no profound differences in either of them? But last night had changed him in some fundamental way. It had changed everything.

Molly unlocked the door. "That'll be fun. It's been awhile since I played, but I used to be a poker and pitch whiz."

"Don't say that to Wilson Formby. He'll try to goad you into putting your money where your mouth is, and he's the luckiest damned poker player I ever sat down at a table with."

"Don't worry. I never play for money. It's not a game anymore, even when only a few dollars are involved. I guess I don't have a gambler's instinct for taking unnecessary risks." As she opened the door, she glanced back at him. He'd come out of the bathroom. He was smiling, but his eyes were intense.

"I always thought my gambling instincts were confined to searching for oil," he muttered. "Until now."

Molly gave him a long look. Then she smiled and tossed a straggling curl out of her eyes. "Risk becomes more acceptable as the stakes go higher, I've always thought. Maybe you should ask yourself when the stakes changed. In your personal life, I mean."

He met her look as he rummaged in a dresser drawer for a clean pair of jeans. "Maybe I should."

Molly stepped into the hall, leaning back into the room with her hand on the knob to say, "Your reluctance makes me think you're afraid of the answer, Chet."

"You still here?" was all he said as he straightened with the jeans in his hand. "I thought you were starving."

"I'll see you at breakfast." She smiled and closed the door on his wary look.

He chuckled to himself. He wasn't afraid of the answer. He *knew* the answer. He just didn't know what to do about it yet.

After putting on the jeans and a shirt, he went to the phone and dialed his uncle's home. Dirk answered sleepily on the fourth ring.

"What time is it?" he grumbled.

"Almost eight."

Dirk groaned. "I didn't get to sleep 'til late. I feel like a herd of cattle spent the night in my mouth."

"You'll feel better when you hear the news. We got a strike, and it looks like a good one. We can't get the pump installed until the rain stops."

Dirk let out a whoop that must have rattled the windows in his bedroom. "There is a God!"

"It sure looks like somebody's looking out for us."

"Whew, this is the best news I've had in a while. We can clear up the outstanding debt on that last well and—"

Dirk halted, and there was a pregnant pause.

"I was under the impression," Chet said, "that we financed that well out of capital on hand."

Dirk expelled a heavy breath. "I didn't want to worry you, Chet. It wasn't as if the note would be called before we could pay it off."

"You found a kindhearted banker?" Chet asked sarcastically.

"In a way. Okay, I gave the Formbys a quarter share, and that cut down our expenses some. They must've sold part of it to some guy in Maine. He called me the other day, wanting to get in on another well."

"Let's get back to the subject at hand," Chet said dryly. "I know all about the guy in Maine. As for the Formbys, giving them a quarter share couldn't have cut down our expenses nearly enough, unless we're paying them a lot more than we were the last time I checked."

"So I borrowed the rest from Suzanne," Dirk said with an edge in his voice. "She brought it up, actually. I hadn't been seeing her for long, but she knew we were good for it. I figured you'd disapprove, so I didn't mention it."

"Great," Chet said. "Don't tell me we're into her for this new well, too."

"No, I went to the bank for that. They'll be glad to hear we've got a new producer. Can I change the subject now?"

"Go ahead."

"Suzanne and I are getting married in September. The new house should be far enough along by then to move into."

"The new house?" Chet asked blankly.

"Didn't I mention that we're having a house built?"

"You know damned well you didn't!" Chet exploded. If the house would be livable by September, it meant it had been under construction for a while, and that meant the wedding had been in the offing long before Dirk came to Sunset.

"Come on, Chet," Dirk cajoled. "I didn't want to shake you up too much all at one time."

"That's baloney. I'm happy you've found some-body. Did you think I wouldn't be?"

"No, no—only, well, after the wedding, I'll want to stay close to home, and that's going to leave you with all the traveling."

Clearly Dirk didn't intend to make the same mis-take with Suzanne that he'd made with Charlotte. Anyway, he was getting older. It was time he slowed down. But if Dirk stayed in Houston, Chet would have to search out and arrange mineral leases in addition to doing the geology work. Instead of being gone only half the time, he would be away from Houston even more.

Chet discovered he didn't like that thought at all. He was honest enough to admit to himself that Molly had a great deal to do with his strong feeling of reluctance, and that confused him. There had been no promises, no commitments. Not in words, anyway, but he had the strange feeling that commitments didn't have to be spoken to be binding.

"Chet, you still there?"

"Yeah, I'm here. Just trying to take it all in."

"I have another bit of news, if you think you can handle any more right now."

"Lay it on me," Chet said with a chuckle.

"That outfit that's been putting out feelers in our direction has stepped up the pressure."

"Monarch Oil?"

"Yeah. Sean Woolery, the chief executive officer, phoned and wants to set up a meeting."

"Sounds like they're ready to make a firm offer," Chet said.

"Yep. I told Sean I'd have to talk to my partner and get back to him. We should know in a week or so what kind of producer we've got out there. If it's as good as it sounds, it should sweeten the deal."

Chet didn't know what to say. It sounded as though Dirk was actually considering selling the company, if the price was right. Yet he'd always sworn he would be at the helm of Delaney Drilling until the day he died.

"It'll be interesting to hear what they have to say," Chet observed cautiously.

"You bet." Dirk sounded relieved. "You know I'd never sell without your complete agreement. Doesn't hurt to listen to them though, does it?"

"Not at all."

"I, well, Chet... Hell, I'll just come out with all of it. Suzanne is after me to retire and... I've been working all my life, and I'm not getting any younger."

Suddenly a light clicked on in Chet's head. Dirk had always said retirement was a dirty word, but Suzanne had changed his mind. *Love* had changed his mind, and that was why he was willing to consider cutting a deal with Woolery. Not that Dirk hadn't earned his retirement, and he deserved his Suzanne and the new house and all the rest of it. It was just that it was a bit much for Chet to absorb all at once.

"Let's see what Woolery has to say," he suggested finally.

"You mean it?"

"Sure."

"'Cause if you don't, it's forgotten."

"No, let's hear what Woolery has in mind."

"Fine, fine. You let me know when you'll be back in Houston, and I'll set it up."

Chet said goodbye and hung up. For a long moment he stood there, gazing at the telephone, thinking that not only had the other shoe finally dropped, but he felt as though he'd been hit by the whole damn shoe store.

Molly found herself humming as she undressed and showered. Yet she wondered if she really had cause for the unexpected feeling of lightheartedness. Chet had been as moved as she by their lovemaking last night, she told herself. There had been a moment when she'd been certain he loved her, and she had willed him to speak the words. But he hadn't.

He seemed determined to steer clear of any commitment. In spite of what he said, she thought his work, which kept him away from home so much, had little to do with it. Other people lived full, happy lives together, despite one or both of them having jobs that required frequent separations. No, it was his childhood experiences that had affected him so deeply.

So deeply, in fact, she thought as she stepped from the shower and reached for a towel, that he might actually walk away from what they had when he left Sunset. She wouldn't make it easy for him, though. If she had to be the one to say "I love you" first, she would. And if he said, "But I don't love you," what then?

Well, then she would have to get on with her life without him—somehow.

She took more care than usual with her makeup, and instead of jeans or shorts, she put on a floral print cotton dress with a flattering scooped neckline and lace trim.

The rain was falling as hard as ever when she left her room for the restaurant. Chet had arrived before her. He sat at the big round table in the corner with Wilson and David Formby and Boney Armbruister. Two other tables were occupied by oil-field workers who lived in other motels, a fourth by some construction workers from town whose jobs had also been rained out for the day. There was no one else in the restaurant. It was the first time since Molly had been working there that the room hadn't been filled by this time of morning.

Chet had saved Molly a chair beside his, and he gave her a long, appreciative smile as she carried her break-fast to the table. "Hey, Molly," Boney greeted her. "We hit pay dirt last night."

"I heard," Molly said, unthinkingly as she seated herself.

Boney seemed disappointed that he'd been cheated of delivering the good news. "I guess Chet told you."

She looked up as a flush started up her throat. She had practically admitted being in Chet's room last night.

"Uh-huh."

Boney appeared puzzled. "When?"

Wilson and David looked at Boney with amuse-ment. "Come on, Boney," Wilson teased. "She was with Chet when David went by his room last night."

"Oh." Boney looked flustered, then became in-tently interested in pouring more maple syrup on his pancakes. Molly kept her eyes lowered and sipped her coffee. It was too late to cover up her blunder now, but she wished they'd drop the subject.

"Wilson . . ." Chet said warningly.

"Hey, I'm sorry, Chet," the man said in feigned apology. "I didn't know it was any big secret or anything. I mean, everybody knows you've been looking after Molly since she got hurt. The way I hear it, you're a regular nursemaid."

Molly gave Chet a pained look. "He's just what the doctor ordered," Wilson said, smiling at Molly over the rim of his cup.

David almost choked on his coffee. He coughed and set his cup down hastily. Wilson pounded his back enthusiastically.

Molly glanced at Boney, who still seemed flustered by his gaffe, and hastened to change the subject. "I'll bet you're eager to go home, Boney. Do you stay with your folks between jobs?"

He gave her a grateful smile. "Yeah. They live on a farm near Amarillo."

"Don't get too comfortable, Boney," David said. "We'll be needing you on that job for Chet and his uncle down south of Garland before long."

"We may have to put that one on hold for a while, David," Chet cut in.

David frowned, and Wilson's head swung around as he looked at Chet in surprise. "How come?"

"I talked to Uncle Dirk a little while ago. He doesn't want to start any new wells immediately."

"Hell, I thought drilling wells was your business," Wilson said. "If you put that well off too long, it'll be winter, and then you might as well wait 'til spring. I can't guarantee David and I will be free then. You can always get somebody else, but—"

"Wilson," Chet interrupted, "I'm going to talk to Uncle Dirk about it when I get back to Houston, and then I'll get in touch with you. I don't know anything for sure yet."

Molly studied Chet curiously. He had something serious on his mind. She'd sensed it ever since she sat down at the table. And it wasn't just the withdrawal that she'd felt in him before she left his room that morning. It was something else. What had he and Dirk talked about?

"Okay," said Wilson, still sounding a bit miffed and more than a little perplexed, "but if we get a firm offer for another job, we'll have to take it."

"I understand that," Chet said as his gaze met Molly's. God, he loved her. For the first time, he wanted to tell her. But he couldn't. Not until he'd come to grips with the changes portended by his conversation with Dirk. Following Chet's gaze, Wilson frowned, then looked at his brother, who shrugged.

Lauren came bounding up to the table at that point, breaking the tension. She hung over Molly's shoulder and peered into her face. "Are you all right now?"

"Right as rain," Molly assured her. She turned sideways in her chair so Lauren could sit on her knee. "No swimming lesson today, huh?"

Lauren looked glum and shook her head. "I can't even go out and play in the rain. Mommy's afraid I'll catch another cold."

"Looks like we're all stuck here," Chet said. "You had your breakfast, Lauren?"

"I ate in the kitchen." She looked around the table expectantly. "What are you all gonna do today?"

Boney pushed his plate back and leaned forward. "Hey, Lauren, you know what we used to do on the farm when we couldn't get out?"

Lauren shook her head solemnly. "What?"

"We'd turn out all the lights and tell ghost stories."

Lauren giggled. "We did that when I slept over at my friend's house." She shivered exaggeratedly. "It was scary—but fun. Let's tell ghost stories!"

The men laughed, and Molly gave Lauren a hug. "You started this, Boney. You go first."

"Gee, I know lots of stories." Boney scratched his chin. "Wait, I've got one. It's about this old guy. He lived out on an oil lease, see, and his job was to keep an eye on the well. Make sure the pumps were all working right, and run off trespassers. Anyway, there was this driller who'd worked on one of the wells, and he got caught in the machinery and died."

"Oooh." Lauren's eyes were wide.

Boney went on, "There was a story around that the driller's ghost haunted one of the wells on that lease, but this old guy didn't believe it. Anyway—"

Molly's attention was more on Lauren than on Boney's story. The little girl's eyes never left Boney. She sat rapt, totally engrossed in the tale. Molly rested her cheek against Lauren's soft hair and felt Chet's hand close around hers beneath the table. Smiling at him, she laced her fingers with his and wished suddenly that they were alone.

Her mind drifted back over the past few days, and she lost track of Boney's story until Lauren suddenly squealed and grabbed Molly's free hand. "That's awful! Wait'll I tell Cassie. It'll gross her out!" She relaxed her grip on Molly's hand. "Tell another one!"

Boney looked shyly around the table, as though suddenly realizing he was the center of attention. "It's David's turn," he said.

"I know some oil field stories, but they're not about ghosts."

"We all know about a hundred of those," said Wilson, laughing.

"Tell one, David," Lauren begged. The other men joined in the chorus.

David held up his hand. "Okay, but it'll be a let-down after Boney's. There's one about this shady operator who made his living selling shares in oil leases. The only problem was, he sold more shares than was honest. Like, he'd sell twenty or thirty one-eighth shares in a single well."

There were groans from the other men.

"Not that old saw," Wilson protested. "Oil men tell that one all over the country and swear they met the shyster once, or somebody who bought one of his worthless shares. But nobody can ever give you a name. It never happened."

"It's oil field mythology," Chet put in.

David looked offended. "Well, you didn't say it had to be true. Boney's story probably never happened, either."

"I want to hear it," Lauren said. "I don't understand what you said about shares."

David picked up the cold biscuit from his plate and broke it into eight pieces, which he arranged in a circle. "Pretend this is a pie, okay? How many pieces are there, Lauren?"

"Eight."

"Right. So what would happen if I brought twenty people in here and gave them each one of these pieces."

"You couldn't, silly," Lauren said. "There are only eight pieces."

"You got it," David said, looking pleased. "If you own an oil lease and you decide to split it up into eight pieces and sell one of them to twenty people, that's against the law. Only you might get away with it, see, because you can't see a piece of an oil lease. All you have is a sheet of paper saying you own one-eighth of a lease, but you have no way of knowing that nineteen other people have those sheets of paper, too. They might never find out unless the well hits and they don't get their money. Understand?"

"I guess so," Lauren said doubtfully.

"Give the kid a break, David," Wilson put in. "She doesn't know what you're talking about."

"I do, too!" Lauren glared at Wilson. "What happened next, David?"

"One time a bunch of investors got together and figured out there were too many of them for the number of shares. Not only that, but when they checked the legal description on their leases, there was no such piece of land. So they went looking for the guy who cheated them. And when they found him, they took him out to a well site and tied him to the top of a derrick and left him there all night. When somebody found him the next morning, he was out of his gourd."

"You mean he went crazy?" Lauren asked, wide-eyed. "That's awful."

"Yeah, but here's the scary part. I've heard that sometimes, at night, guys working a well—it can be anyplace in the world—have seen the hazy figure of a man hanging from the top of a derrick."

"Wow," Lauren breathed.

"I think that's enough goose bumps for now," Molly said.

"I agree," Chet said.

"Let's play cards," Wilson suggested, perking up.

"I've got Monopoly," Lauren put in.

"Well, go get it," Molly said, ignoring Wilson, who was grimacing and rolling his eyes.

Lauren jumped down and ran out of the restaurant. "Monopoly," Wilson groaned.

"Aw, be a sport," Boney said.

Just then Jude came into the restaurant from the lobby. She looked around with a little frown, spotted Molly and came to the table. "Molly, there's a police officer on the phone. He wants to talk to you."

Molly looked up, startled. She was aware of four pairs of eyes trained on her face. She glanced at Chet, who gave a barely perceptible nod, and excused herself.

The telephone receiver lay on the desk in the small office, and she gingerly picked it up. "Hello?"

"Molly Sinclair?"

"Yes."

"This is Officer Handy of the Sunset Police Department. I spoke to Mr. Delaney the other night."

"Yes, he told me. Have you learned something about the hit-and-run?"

"No, ma'am. We've talked to everybody on that block, and nobody saw or even heard it. I just wanted to let you know we'd followed up on it."

"Oh." Molly wasn't really surprised; nevertheless, she felt disappointed. "I appreciate that. Thank you, Officer."

"You're quite welcome, ma'am. If you remember anything about that car, let us know."

She hung up and left the office. Jude was waiting just outside the door. Chet was with her.

"I'm sure it was the right thing to do," Jude was saying. She turned quickly at the sound of the office door opening. "Chet says he talked to the police about the car that hit you, Molly."

"That was Officer Handy," Molly said, meeting Chet's tense look. "They questioned the people on the block, but nobody saw anything. There's nothing else they can do."

"You didn't even get a glimpse of the car?" Jude asked.

Molly shivered with a sudden chill and hugged herself as she shook her head. Chet put a protective arm around her. "You okay?"

She managed a smile. "Sure."

Jude pursed her lips thoughtfully as she looked from Chet to Molly. "How come I'm getting the feeling you two haven't told me all you know about that accident?"

"But we have," Molly said.

"Okay, only I still say there's something strange going on here," Jude said. "I'd like to help, if I can."

"There's nothing—" Molly began.

"Molly," Chet interjected, "we can trust Jude. I think we should tell her what's going on. I'd feel a whole lot better if she knew."

Molly's first instinct was to refuse. But on quick reflection, she thought perhaps Chet was right. Jude, of all the people she'd met in Sunset, could be trusted.

Jude searched their faces, then asked, "Knew what?"

"Let's go in the office and close the door," Molly suggested. "So we can talk in private."

Chapter 13

After hesitating in the doorway a moment, Chet said, "I'll leave the two of you alone." He went out, closing the door behind him.

Frowning, Jude watched Molly settle in a half sitting position on the desk.

Molly was suddenly aware of the silence in the office. Sometime during the last few minutes, the rain had stopped.

She met Jude's puzzled gaze and said, "George Backus was my father."

"George was—?" Shock flooded Jude's face, and she lowered herself into a chair. "You're Lala? Good heavens, Molly! I don't understand any of this."

"I guess I should start from the beginning," Molly said. "You see, Dad wrote to me the day before he died." She went on to tell Jude of her growing conviction that her father's death was somehow connected to the letter's incomprehensible last lines, and about her subsequent decision to come to Sunset. She held back nothing except the nightmare in which Dirk Delaney had been behind the wheel of the car that hit her. She hadn't even confided that particular detail to Chet. When she let herself dwell on it, the dream's ending still troubled her, but it proved nothing, and Dirk was back in Houston now.

Jude listened intently, her expression shifting from surprise to amazement to dismay. "So you never intended staying here for long. Even when I hired you."

"I'm sorry I deceived you," Molly said, "I just didn't know any other way to find out the truth."

Jude still looked miffed. "What does Chet think?"

"At first he thought I was wrong," Molly admitted. "That Dad's death was an accident, pure and simple. Since the hit-and-run..." She gestured broadly, not really sure that Chet had done a complete about-face. He was concerned for her and simply didn't want her taking unnecessary risks. "He's rethinking his position."

Jude shook her head, clearly finding it difficult to digest all that Molly had told her. "I don't know. It all sounds so incredible."

"I know. It took two months for me to decide my suspicions were even worth pursuing." She shrugged helplessly. "And at this point, I don't know any more than when I started."

"Maybe you should give it up," Jude said kindly. "Go home and try to forget it. You'll have to go soon, anyway."

"You sound like Chet. I think the two of you want to get rid of me."

"Chet's worried about you. Now that I know the whole story, so am I." Jude laughed shortly. "And I'm put out with you, too. But I don't want to be responsible for keeping you here if something else happens. Though Lord knows what I'll do without you 'til Mae is able to come back. But that'll only be a couple of weeks."

"I'll stay until then." In two weeks, work on the Delaney well would be completed. Chet and the others would be gone. Molly didn't know what her life would be like then; she only knew that, after Chet, it could never be the same.

In two days the ground at the well site was dry enough for the men to return to work. Before leaving that morning, Chet came to Molly's room to say he wanted to come back during her afternoon break, if she could wait that long to have lunch with him.

In her nightgown, she stood half behind the door and smiled at him, her eyes still languid from sleep. "I'll wait. Would you like to come in?"

"I can't now," he said regretfully, reaching out to touch her tousled black curls. "I'm sorry I woke you."

"I needed to get up anyway."

"Do you have to leave the motel while I'm gone?"

"No, and stop worrying."

"I will—when you're safely out of here."

"That will be in two weeks. I've already told Jude."

He gave her a long, steady look. "All right. In the meantime..."

"I'll watch my back," she finished ruefully. "Now, about lunch. I'll fix a tray. We can eat here."

"Good idea." He gave her a quick kiss on the nose and was gone.

After closing the door, Molly engaged the night chain and wandered into the bathroom. Before stepping into the shower, she stripped off the tape that still bound her right side. Except for an occasional twinge at a sudden movement, the pain was gone.

As she stepped beneath the shower's spray, her thoughts flew past the next few hours to the late lunch with Chet in her room. She experienced a feeling of urgency, as if everything in her life were coming to a head. Maybe it was time to lay all her cards on the table.

At 2:00 p.m. she began arranging the meal on a large tray in the kitchen. Elsie was busy in the pantry, checking off items for the dinner menu.

Jude watched Molly set out two plates and two sets of silverware. "Lunching in your room?" she asked.

Molly sliced two helpings of roast beef. "Uh-huh."

Jude seemed her usual friendly self today. Apparently she had forgiven Molly for deceiving her.

"Expecting company, are you?"

Molly gave her a half smile. "Chet's joining me."

"I see," Jude observed wryly.

"You can deduct the extra meal from my wages."

"An extra slice of roast beef and a few vegetables? Don't be ridiculous." Jude pulled a ring of keys from her pocket, opened a corner cabinet and selected a bottle of Cabernet Sauvignon. She handed it to Molly.

Molly lifted a brow. "What's the occasion?"

"I was hoping you'd tell me," Jude said with a grin. Molly eyed her warily. "No, huh? Well, just call it a feeling. Or, if you prefer, a generous impulse."

"Thank you. I'm glad you're not still mad at me," said Molly as she set the wine and two stemmed glasses on the tray.

Jude continued to watch her for a moment, then glanced quickly toward the pantry and lowered her voice. "I've thought a lot about your father the past two days. He was a good, kind man."

"Yes," Molly agreed. "He was the only family I had. I miss him terribly."

"It will hurt less, in time," Jude sympathized.

"I'm sure you're right. It would be easier, though, if I knew what really happened." She folded two cloth napkins and laid them on the tray. "Jude, did you have any indication that he was drinking, those last few days?"

Jude eyed her sadly. "I've asked myself the same question, and the answer is no. I never saw him take a drink, never smelled alcohol on him. I never would have let Lauren go with him if I'd thought any such thing." She paused, then added gently, "That doesn't necessarily prove he wasn't having a few on the job."

True, Molly admitted. In fact, Wilson had smelled alcohol on her father a couple of times. "Did he seem different—worried, or unusually preoccupied?"

"Not really. I think he was disappointed about the well."

Molly looked at her sharply. "He told you that?"

"Not in so many words."

"What *did* he say, Jude?"

"The last night he was here before…well, before he died, he came in the kitchen. Everybody else had gone, and I was making out a grocery list at the table. I asked if he needed something. He said no, he was restless, couldn't sleep." Jude frowned for an instant, thinking. "I remember he made himself a cup of hot tea, and then he said he didn't think he'd be here much longer, and that he was going to miss us, especially Lauren."

"So he already knew the well wasn't going to be a producer. He'd decided to recommend plugging."

Jude hesitated. "He didn't say that exactly. What he said was, 'Jude, I think they're going to plug my well.' I didn't think anything of it at the time, but now that I think of it, it does seem an odd way of putting it."

"And that's all he said?"

Jude nodded. "I said something like, 'Oh, that's too bad.' He was already leaving the kitchen to go back to his room with his tea, and he didn't answer."

"It does sound strange—like his last letter—as if the decision to suspend drilling was out of his hands."

"Wasn't it?"

"Not completely. In fact, the geologist's advice is almost always taken, and Dad's last report recommended plugging the well." Molly sighed. "I don't know. Maybe I'm reading hidden meanings into perfectly innocent remarks."

"I wish I could help put your mind at rest," Jude said.

"Distance will do that, I suppose, and time." Molly picked up the tray. "I'll see you at five, and thanks for the wine."

Chet arrived at the room only moments after Molly. She had set the lamp on the floor and pulled out the bedside table, arranging the plates and silverware on it. She let Chet in, and his eyes lit up at the sight of her.

He kissed her hungrily before she stepped back and turned her attention to dishing up the food. "Why don't you pour the wine?"

He gave her a curious look before lifting the bottle. He studied the label. "Very nice. What's the occasion?"

Molly laughed, her back to him. "Exactly what I asked Jude when she gave it to me. She said it was a generous impulse." She felt stiff and uncertain. This wasn't going to be as easy as she'd imagined. She almost wished she hadn't suggested they eat in her room.

Oddly enough, it felt as if this was their first time alone together. But it wasn't being alone with him that made her feel so nervous. It was what she had decided that morning to tell him. Now that he was here, she doubted the wisdom of that decision. It might sound to him as if she were issuing an all-or-nothing ultimatum. But it was a risk she had to take. First, though, she had to get through the meal.

He popped the cork and poured. "Thank God for generous impulses." He handed a glass to Molly as she sat on the side of the bed, leaving the rocker for him.

He lowered himself into the chair. There was something different about Molly. He couldn't quite put his finger on it, but he sensed a tension in her that kept him at arm's length. He wondered if the date she had set for leaving Sunset had anything to do with it.

Outwardly she seemed relaxed enough, smiling at him as she lifted her wineglass. But underneath she was edgy, and her eyes were more intent than he'd ever seen them, as though she were dissecting him. As if they hadn't talked together, shared the same bed, been as intimate as a man and woman could be.

He felt the warmth of the wine enter his blood-stream, but he couldn't relax. There was a purpose in Molly that hadn't been there before. This was more than a simple lunch.

"How was your morning?" he asked.

"Busy." She set down the glass and reached for her fork. What a polite conversation we're having, she thought in dismay as she met his look. "And yours?" She knew she sounded inane, but she couldn't seem to stop herself.

"Busy," he said dryly.

She took a small bite of meat and put her fork down. "Do you know how much longer you'll be at the site?"

"Not precisely. A week, or so."

Moistening her lips, she searched for another topic. "Jude told me something odd today. Something my father said to her the night before he died."

"Oh?"

"He said they were going to plug his well."

"They who?"

"He didn't say, but don't you think it's odd?"

He remained thoughtful for a moment. "He was probably just referring to the hands. The geologist makes the recommendations, he doesn't do the actual physical work." He shrugged as he poured more wine. "I wouldn't have used those words, but they aren't ex-actly sinister."

Her eyes swiftly met his. "Is that what you think I'm implying?"

"I didn't say that."

She took a quick swallow of wine. "It's what you meant, though, isn't it?"

"Do you really want to know?"

Annoyed, she stabbed a carrot slice with her fork. "You shouldn't even have to ask. I want you to be honest with me. Haven't we come that far in our relationship?"

He cut a bite of meat and ate it slowly, then lifted his glass and took a long, hard look at the red liquid but didn't taste it. "All right. I think you're trying to dredge up every shred of information about your father's words and actions before he died, and you're turning the most insignificant things into momentous clues. Is that honest enough for you?"

She lifted her wine and swallowed, then said stiffly, "Yes."

"I'm not saying you don't have every right to ask your questions, Molly. I just don't want to fight with you."

She knew it must seem that she was trying to pick a fight. She was being too defensive. "I don't want that, either. So let's just finish our lunch."

"Agreed," he said. He had been looking forward to being with her, but his very presence seemed to put her on edge. Maybe she was just having a bad day. Molly was entitled to her moods, like everybody else. Regretfully, he decided the wisest course would be to finish lunch as quickly as common decency allowed and return to the site.

At length he dropped his napkin on the small table and stood. "I need to get back to the well."

A quick look of vulnerability flickered in her gray eyes as she rose to face him. "So soon?" She seemed to regret the words the instant they were out, and she turned away from him.

"I got the impression that's what you wanted." He would have touched her then, but somehow the distance between them was too great. "Isn't it?"

"No—I don't know." She dragged a hand through her hair, her back still to him. "This isn't going the way I expected."

He felt awkward, and angry with her for making him feel that way. "Perhaps if I knew what you expected...."

She spun around. "This is very difficult for me, Chet, so don't be patronizing." She fumbled for the words that would make things right. "Look, this isn't going to work right now. Could we talk about it later, please?"

"No, I don't think so." He took a step toward her, then hesitated as she bit her bottom lip. When had everything changed between them? She had always been so open and giving, so willing to expose her vulnerability to him. Now she was drawing back, and that hurt. More than he'd ever thought he could be hurt. "I don't mean to patronize you, Molly," he said in a low voice. "But I don't know what you want. Why don't you spell it out for me?"

"I thought it would be so easy!" she cried, surprising herself with her own vehemence. "I thought we'd have lunch and relax and just talk—really talk, I mean. And then the right moment would come... Damn it, Chet, I planned exactly how I'd say it."

"It must be some momentous announcement, whatever it is," he murmured, then gave a short laugh before he stepped to the door. "Because you're afraid to say it to my face."

"No. I'm afraid of what I'll see in your eyes. I'm not prepared for that." He halted at the door, waiting. "I guess I'm not as strong as I thought. If I can't see your eyes... No, don't turn around. Stay like that, Chet, please." She took a deep breath. "I can say it now, and you'll just have to handle it. I'm in love with you."

Chet froze, his hand on the doorknob. He had expected something devastating. Something terrible and painful. Not this, though it was painful in its own way. Because he'd been kidding himself that what had happened between them, no matter how profoundly he'd been moved by it, had stopped short of love. That his own feelings of love weren't real, just a momentary response that would soon be gone.

He was honest enough to admit that Molly had affected him deeply, but somehow he'd convinced himself that her feelings for him were more vague, that they were all tangled up with grieving for her father and the need for solace. He'd been hanging on to that convoluted line of reasoning to keep from dealing with his own feelings. Her bald declaration had torn that comforting shield away from him.

Wordlessly, he turned to face her. They watched each other, both wary, their eyes intense with what seemed more like fear than any tender emotion.

He'd had no idea, Molly thought. She had made a disastrous miscalculation, and she would have given anything to relive the last few minutes, to make the scene come out differently.

"I can see you're overjoyed to hear it." Furious with herself for thinking that one of them had to utter the words before they parted or somehow it would be too late, she snatched up her half-empty wineglass from the table and drained it. Even if he didn't respond in kind, she'd told herself, she would at least know that she'd been completely honest with him. Too late she thought that perhaps honesty wasn't all it was cracked up to be.

She felt calmer when she set the glass down. Never had she imagined that silence could be so painful. But it would not kill her. She could accept the pain, and it would not destroy her. "I could say I was only kidding, but I don't think you'd buy it." Her lips formed a bitter smile. "Oh, well, I'm sure I'm not the first woman to throw herself at you. What do you say to them? That the timing isn't right? That you're very fond of them, but—"

"Stop." Chet ran a hand over his face. "I wasn't expecting this. I don't know what to say."

She turned her back to him and squeezed her eyes shut for a moment. "Good bye would be appropriate."

"Molly, no! I've hurt you— Hell, I'm bungling this royally. You scare me, honey. You've always scared me. This kind of thing is easier for women—for you. You've done it before."

She whirled around. "Done it before!" she exploded. "What the hell does that mean?"

"You've been in love before. That's all I meant." Molly was pale, but her eyes were darker and angrier than he'd ever seen them. Then they filled with tears.

"Not like this," she said defiantly.

Suddenly, painfully, he needed her—the softness, the vulnerability, the fire. "Molly," he murmured as he reached for her. At first her body was stiff in his arms.

Whispering her name, he traced kisses over her face, tasting her tears. Again and again, he returned to her lips until he felt her response. "I need you, Molly." Pressing his mouth to hers, he let his tongue convey his hunger.

With a deep sigh of pleasure, her response grew stronger. He needed her. He could admit that. But why couldn't he say he loved her?

Perhaps because he didn't.

She dragged herself away with a cry of alarm, aware that her heart was pounding with a combination of anger and desire. "Chet! I don't want this. I hate it!"

"It didn't feel like hate," he said quietly. Clasping her shoulders, he drew her close again.

"It isn't fair."

His mouth silenced her. Slowly he slid his hands down her back to cup her hips. She was warm and soft, and his need to lose himself in her roared in his blood. Gently he laid her back across the bed, coming down atop her, and then his mouth was on hers again.

Had it ever been like this before? Molly wondered dazedly as he moved his lips and hands over her with tender confidence. Had his lovemaking ever been so sweet and so painful at the same time? He savored the taste of her mouth, the taste of her skin, and murmured his pleasure.

Steeped in the heat and scent of him, she could find no strength to push him away. He knew how to pleasure her, and by doing so he was returning things to the way they had been. Need, want, sex, but no promises, no commitments. She had gambled everything, and she had lost. And still she was being drawn back into his spell. But inside her there was a core of emptiness that hadn't been there before.

She squeezed her eyes closed for a moment as she gathered her strength. "Chet," she whispered. "No, Chet, not like this. I can't."

He lifted his head, staring at her with eyes dark and dazed by passion. "Molly, honey, I want you so much...."

"I know you do," she murmured. "And I want you. But that isn't enough anymore."

He shut his eyes for an instant, surprised at how much pain her rejection could bring. Then he gave a quick, hard laugh. "This is a hell of a time to raise the stakes."

"I think I did that earlier," she said, struggling for control. "You just chose to ignore it."

Distressed by the determination in her quiet words, he pushed himself off the bed. "I have things to say to you, but you can't expect me to say them now."

She gazed up at him, her eyes full of love and sadness. "I don't expect anything. When I said I love you, I was simply stating a fact. I wasn't asking for more than you're willing to give in return. If it seemed that way, I'm sorry."

His eyes stung as he turned away from her. She hadn't asked for more than he could give, but she would no longer accept less than all of him. She loved him, but she could send him away, even as the hurt of doing so tore at her. Love, he realized helplessly, could not be denied or put on hold.

"I wish I could be what you want," he said huskily, his hand on the door. "I'm sorry."

She swallowed, temporarily winning the battle with tears. "There's nothing to apologize for. We are what we are, both of us."

He left it at that. In the empty silence, she stared at the closed door.

Chapter 14

For nearly a week, Chet was polite but cautious, keeping his distance. He made no effort to see Molly alone.

He was closed to her. She had pushed him away. For six days, she awoke every morning with the same thought: she'd lost Chet. She had laid her cards on the table, and he hadn't liked the stakes. He had chosen not to play.

It was for the best. She told herself that a dozen times each day, struggling to convince herself. At first she hung on to the one thing he'd told her that held any hope: *I have things to say to you.* She told herself he was thinking it through and would come to her when he was ready. But by the end of a week, she could no longer believe that. She had known the risk she was taking, and she had to learn to live with the consequences.

Molly began to count the days until Mae could return to work and she could go back to Dallas. She would conquer the pain of Chet's rejection more quickly if she didn't have to see him every day.

There was a part of her that would always love him, but she couldn't regret what had happened between them. She had given her love freely, without conditions or expectations. Love, even when it wasn't returned, was never wrong. It was to be cherished always, along with the memories Chet had given her.

The sun still came up every morning. She was alone, but she was young and healthy, and she had work that she loved. It was more than many people had. From these things, she could make a life.

At length a calmness settled over her. She managed to talk to Chet in the restaurant as easily as she talked to the other men, at least on the surface. She congratulated herself on her strength and dignity.

Then one morning, after she'd eaten breakfast and was returning to her room, she found Chet leaning against the wall near her door, waiting patiently. All the hard-won strength and dignity rushed out of her, and her heart raced frantically until she thought it would burst. Holding herself together, she stopped a few feet from him.

"Molly," he murmured, "I've been waiting for you."

"Yes?" She tried to gather the thoughts tumbling through her mind.

He walked toward her, but stopped short of touching her. His eyes were grave, his expression tense. "I have to talk to you. Can I see you this evening? Your room, my room—or we could go for a drive. Wherever you say."

"Well, I . . . Yes, of course."

A little of his tension seemed to ease. "I'll see you then."

Before Molly could speak, she was alone in the hallway.

For the rest of the day she was a bundle of raw-edged nerves. What would Chet say to her? That he loved her and wanted her with him always? That he loved her but couldn't make a commitment to her? That he didn't love her at all? One minute her heart soared in joyful anticipation; the next it plummeted into depression.

At four that afternoon she was lying on her bed, trying to relax before her dinner shift started at five. Unable to nap, she kept glancing at the clock every few moments, wondering if it had stopped. She wanted only to finish the shift and meet Chet. Whatever he planned to say, she wanted to get it over with.

The ring of the telephone set every nerve in her body on end. She grabbed the receiver. "Hello."

"Molly? It's Wilson Formby."

His voice sounded strained. Molly sat up. "Wilson, where are you?"

"Out at the site. It's Chet."

Alarm shot through her. "What's wrong?"

"He's been hurt."

"Oh my God! How badly? Will he be all right?"

"I don't know. He was helping us put in the new pump, and the damn thing must have been damaged. It broke. Just flew apart and something hit Chet and—"

Molly gripped the receiver as though it were a life preserver. "Where is he?" she interrupted.

"Here. We called an ambulance to take him to the hospital."

"What hospital?"

"Er . . . Snyder, I guess. Molly, he keeps asking for you. If you hurry, you can make it out here before the ambulance."

"I'm on my way." She slammed down the receiver and snatched up her purse. Rummaging inside for her car keys, she ran down the hall past Ingrid, who was on the telephone at the cashier's desk.

"Tell Jude I've gone out to the well site," she called over her shoulder. "Chet's been hurt, and they've called an ambulance. From there I'll go on to the hospital. I don't know when I'll be back."

She found the keys as she reached her car. Her hands were shaking so badly, she made several tries at unlocking the door before she accomplished it. Then she fell onto the sunbaked seat and immediately felt the heat from the upholstery penetrate the back of her blouse and skirt.

She stabbed the key at the ignition, made contact on the second attempt, and started the engine. Her breath was coming in gulps and gasps. Gripping the steering wheel, she tried to steady herself before driving out of the parking lot.

Get hold of yourself, Molly, she ordered silently. You won't be any good to Chet if you wreck this car. After a moment, she slowly relaxed her grip and put the car in gear.

As she drove out of town, she prayed over and over: let him be all right. Please, dear God, let him be all right.

Driving the few miles from town to the well site was like struggling to surface from a nightmare. Between snatches of prayer, horrible images flitted through her mind. Images of Chet hurt, maimed, dead.

After what seemed like hours she saw the turnoff and whipped toward it, going too fast. The car left the paved highway and spun half around, throwing gravel in all directions. Molly slammed on the brakes and came to a stop, facing the way she'd come. Stunned, she sat in the ensuing silence for a few moments, still clasping the steering wheel with all her might.

Then, carefully, she eased off the brake and backed the car enough to turn it in the right direction. "Oh God, let him be all right," she whispered as she drove down the lane to the site.

Wilson's car was parked between the trailers, but Chet's was nowhere in sight. The ambulance must have come and gone, and Wilson or Boney had followed it in Chet's car. But if both Wilson and Boney had gone, they would have left her a note.

She pulled in beside Wilson's car and leaped out. As she ran toward the trailers, Wilson stepped out of the doghouse.

"Molly."

She ran up the steps. "Has the ambulance taken him? How is he?"

"They just left. He was conscious, Molly. Try to calm down."

"Did they take him to Snyder?"

"Yes."

"Boney must have driven Chet's car."

"Oh—yes."

She spun around and started back down the steps. "I'm going to the hospital."

Wilson followed her and took her arm. "Not 'til you're calmer. Come on inside the trailer and let me get you something to drink."

She tried to pull away, but he held on to her. "Let me go, Wilson! I have to see Chet."

"They'll take care of him. Molly, please, come inside. You're too upset to drive right now."

Her face was hot, and her head throbbed. She was frantic with fear. Wilson was right. She knew he was right. "Only for a few minutes," she said and let him lead her back up the steps.

Cool air hit her as they stepped into the air-conditioned trailer. Wilson closed the door and sat her down on the couch. Leaning back, she closed her eyes and heard the plop of ice cubes into a glass and the soft fizzing sound as he poured a soft drink.

"Here." He placed the drink in her hand.

She opened her eyes. "Thanks, Wilson." She took a sip. "Are you sure he was conscious when they took him?"

"Positive."

"Was he coherent?"

"Yes. Honestly. I'm not just saying it to make you feel better."

"Tell me what happened."

He stood in front of the refrigerator, next to the narrow counter that ran along one wall of the trailer. He gripped the edge of the counter. "That pump must have been faulty when it left the plant, or it was damaged in shipment. But it looked okay. Boney and I were trying to install it, and we needed another pair of hands, so Chet came out to help us. That's when a piece flew off the damn thing and hit Chet in the back of the head.''

"His head!" Molly sat forward abruptly, "Oh God, he could have been seriously hurt." She set her drink on the floor and stood. "I can't stay here any longer. I have to go. I have to see him for myself."

Wilson strode to her and, placing his hands on her shoulders, pushed her back down on the couch. "Finish your drink first."

She stared up at him. His tone had hardened. Was it anxiety or—?

"Your drink, Molly. Finish it and I won't delay you any longer."

Of course it was only anxiety. She took a deep breath and pressed two fingers against the bridge of her nose in an effort to ease her tension headache. She had to get a grip on herself if she was going to drive all the way to Snyder. She would be no good to Chet if she drove her car into a ditch. She managed a feeble smile and reached for her glass. Her hand was shaking.

She found she didn't really want a cold drink, after all. The cola had a bitter taste. After a single swallow, she set the glass down again. "Thank you for being so concerned for me, Wilson, but I really have to go." She stood. "I won't be able to calm down until I know that Chet will be all right. I'll drive carefully. I promise."

His back to her, Wilson opened a drawer beneath the counter. As he turned around, he stepped in front of the door.

"Sorry, Molly, but I can't let you go." He had a gun in his hand.

Chet drove ten miles on the road to Snyder before he found a service station. He pulled in. "I have to make a phone call, Boney."

Boney got out of the car, too. "Think I'll get a root beer. You want something?"

"Cream soda, if they have it." As Boney entered the station, Chet went into the public phone booth outside.

The pump had arrived at the well site by truck at noon. Wilson and Boney had spent several hours working with it and finally discovered that one small piece was missing. Wilson had thought the welding shop in Snyder could make a substitute piece, and he had volunteered to stay at the site and do as much as could be done without the missing piece so they could finish the job the next day.

Boney could have made the trip alone in Chet's car, but Chet hadn't quite trusted Boney's ability to describe to the welder what they needed. To be sure the job was done right, he'd felt he had to go, too.

He'd realized after he'd left the site that they would be late getting back to Sunset. He didn't want Molly to be sitting in her room after her evening shift, waiting for him. He dropped some coins into the phone slot and dialed the motel. When Ingrid answered, he asked to speak to Molly.

"She's not here."

"This is Chet, Ingrid. Where is she?"

"Chet? It didn't sound like you. Hey, are you calling from the hospital or what?"

"Hospital! Why would you think that?"

"Well, 'cause when Molly left here she said you'd been hurt out at the well site and she was going to try to get there before the ambulance came and... Are you okay, Chet? What happened?"

"Nothing happened. I'm not hurt. Where did Molly get that idea?"

"Gosh, I don't know, but she ran out of here like a bat out of hell. She had a phone call right before. I noticed the button for the line in her room was lit up. Maybe somebody played a practical joke on her."

"Yeah." Chet felt the hairs on the back of his neck stand up. "Thanks, Ingrid." He hung up and immediately dialed the Sunset police. He told the dispatcher that Molly Sinclair might be in danger at the Delaney well site in the Sunset field. He demanded that an officer be dispatched immediately to check on her.

He slammed the receiver on its hook and raced back to the car as Boney sauntered out of the station carrying two soft drink cans.

"Get in!" Chet yelled. "We're going back to the well site."

"What's up?" Boney asked as Chet gunned the motor and roared away from the station.

Chet repeated his conversation with Ingrid.

"If somebody called her from the site, it had to be Wilson," Boney said in a puzzled tone. "You reckon it's like Ingrid said, his idea of a joke?"

"I hope so," Chet said grimly.

"What else could it be?"

"I don't know." Chet's mind reeled with frightening questions. He should have suspected Wilson, he had never really believed that Dirk could be involved.

What if that piece of pump hadn't been missing? What if Wilson had taken it and volunteered to stay at the site while Chet and Boney went to Snyder, and then had lured Molly out there? But why? In God's name, why?

"You better slow down, boss," Boney said.

Chet brought his mind back to his driving and saw the speedometer needle hovering near eighty. He slowed to sixty-five. "If he hurts her, I'll kill him."

Boney stared at him. "Who? Wilson? You mean because she wouldn't go out with him? Aw, that's like water off a duck's back to Wilson. He wouldn't hurt her."

Chet did not respond or relax his grip on the wheel.

"I'm sorry it had to come to this, Molly."

She discovered that her knees were too weak to hold her and sank down on the couch. "It was you," she whispered incredulously.

He dropped his arm so that the gun pointed at the floor, but he watched her alertly, and he was still blocking the trailer's only exit. "I tried to scare you off the other night while you were out running, but you didn't take the hint."

"David told you I'm George Backus's daughter."

He shrugged negligently.

"He's in it with you, then?"

His mouth twisted in an ironic smile. "Dave? No way. He's too big a coward to engage in 'questionable' business practices."

Molly stared at him. Questionable business practices?

"Don't look so innocent, Molly. You've suspected ever since Abernathy called the motel that there might be too many like him."

She stared at him as scraps of memory began to snap together to form a pattern. She remembered David's innocent tale about oil-field shysters who oversold shares in a well. She remembered how Wilson had brushed off the story as legendary. "You oversold the well my father worked on."

He laughed shortly. "A wee bit."

She came to her feet then and took a defiant step toward him. "My father found out, and you killed him!"

The gun came up, stopping her. "We're leaving here, as soon as you finish your drink." He gestured with the gun. "Go on. Pick it up."

He was going to kill her. Resignation crept over her, bringing an odd calmness with it. She bent and picked up the glass. Why did he want her to drink it before he killed her? He had to be crazy. Watching him, she raised the glass slowly.

"Hurry up!" he ordered.

She touched her lips to the rim of the glass and tilted it. She tasted the bitter cola, and at last she understood. David had said Wilson had sleeping pills. He'd drugged her drink. She spat the mouthful of cola back into the glass.

He stiffened, and suddenly she was staring down the barrel of the gun. "Damn it, I said drink it!"

He wanted her drugged so that she would be more manageable, but she wouldn't make it easy for him. She was quaking inside as she said, "No."

Fury contorted his face. Molly closed her eyes, expecting to die on the spot. Then the sound of a siren split the silence.

Wilson jerked his head toward the window in the trailer door. Color drained from his face. In the seconds that his attention was off her, Molly edged closer to a window.

A police car stopped several hundred yards from the trailers, and the shriek of the siren was cut off. An officer scrambled out on the far side of the vehicle, gun in hand. Then Chet's car hurtled down the lane and stopped behind the police car.

The officer gestured frantically for Chet and Boney to get down as they climbed out of the car. "You—in those trailers!" the officer shouted. "Come out with your hands up."

Molly didn't know if Chet and the police understood the situation or were simply being extremely cautious. She didn't even know how they'd known to come there. But at that point she had nothing to lose. "Chet, Wilson's got a gun!" she shouted.

Wilson whirled on her and shoved her against the couch. "Shut up, damn you!"

Meeting his furious look, she deliberately turned her glass up and poured the drink on the floor. "It's drugged," she observed quietly. "Like the drink you gave my father. That's why he was staggering when he left that day. You'd already planted that half-full whiskey bottle in his trailer, just to make sure everybody would assume he was drunk."

"I said shut up," he grated and glanced out the window again.

Molly sank back on the couch. "Do you really want to shoot me and be tried for two murders?"

He glared at her, his eyes narrowing as he considered his options.

"When you realized the well would be a producer, you typed the report recommending plugging and forced my father to sign it."

"I played the odds—nine to one—that it would be a dry hole, and I lost. So I had to make sure the Delaneys didn't find out. Yeah, I made George sign that report. I couldn't let the investors I'd sold shares to find out they'd been bilked."

He stared at her stonily while his mind scurried frantically for a way out.

"What I don't understand," she went on, "is why you were willing to gamble that he'd pass out and go off the road just as he reached the lake."

"It was no gamble," he snarled. "I followed his car to the highway. He was already losing consciousness by then. I drove the car to the lake and ran back here. It took about five minutes."

And then he told the other men that he'd tried to catch up with her father but failed, Molly thought. They'd had no reason to doubt him.

"I didn't count on your old man writing to you about his suspicions. He figured out the well had been oversold, but he thought the Delaneys had done it. I had to stop him before he accused them to their faces. I didn't want to kill him, but I couldn't bribe him, so..." He looked at the gun in his hand as though suddenly wondering what it was doing there. Then he seemed to gather himself together. "George was stubborn as a mule, like you. If you hadn't come here, if you'd just let it alone, no one would ever have known."

"I'm glad I didn't let it alone," she told him, "even if you kill me."

"Formby, come out with your hands up!" The police officer was using a megaphone. The command boomed through the trailer with authority.

"Give up, Wilson," Molly pleaded. "You can't get away now."

"The hell I will!" His arm shot out, and he dragged her to her feet. Holding her in front of him, he shoved her to the door. "Open it."

She turned the knob, and the door swung open slowly. "Don't shoot!" Boney shouted. "He's got Molly in front of him!"

"I'll kill her if anybody tries to stop me!" Wilson yelled as he shoved her down the steps.

Molly's eyes darted everywhere, searching for Chet. She couldn't see him or the other two men now. All three must be crouched behind the cars. Wilson hesitated for a moment at the bottom of the steps, then dragged Molly toward his car between the trailers. In that moment of hesitation, he'd clearly been deciding whether to take his own car or Chet's, which would be easier to get to. He'd opted for his own, and that was his fatal mistake.

As he backed around the end of the trailer, dragging Molly with him, he exposed his back. Chet, who was hiding behind the trailer, stepped out and brought a tire iron down on Wilson's head. Wilson dropped, and the gun tumbled from his hand. The officer rushed forward, snatched up the gun and whirled to keep Wilson in shooting range. But Wilson was out cold.

Molly felt the blood leave her face, and her knees buckled. "Chet?" she murmured as she fell into his arms.

"Molly!" His voice broke. "Oh, Molly, sweetheart, I love you."

Chapter 15

"Tell me again," Molly said. She was held tightly in Chet's arms, her head nestled on his shoulder. They were seated on the couch in his trailer. He hadn't stopped holding her since she'd fallen into his arms outside.

Wilson had been handcuffed and taken to the police station. Boney had driven Wilson's car to town so he could break the news to David. Chet had said that he and Molly would follow as soon as she was all right.

After that one instant when she'd nearly fainted and then had felt Chet's strong arms around her, bearing her up, she had been more than all right. She'd told him about Wilson's phone call and her mad dash to the site, thinking he'd been hurt. He'd told her about calling the motel and then the police before he'd driven back to the site.

Molly tilted her head to look up at him. "I want to hear you say the words again," she prodded him.

He laughed, and his lips found hers. With a groan of relief, of joy, he drew her down until they lay on the couch. "What words?"

Framing his face with her hands, Molly looked down at him with serious eyes. "The words you said to me right after you hit Wilson."

"I love you," he whispered, then let out a long shuddering breath. "God, how I love you, Molly. When I thought he was going to hurt you..." Unable to finish, he pulled her head down for a long kiss.

Molly sighed and snuggled against him. "How long have you known?"

He stroked her hair. "For weeks."

She lifted her head. "You mean you knew the night I told you? And you let me agonize for a week?"

Taking her hand, he pressed his lips to the palm. "I couldn't get the words out then. I was afraid to face how I felt. I hurt you, didn't I?"

"Yes, you did."

"I'm sorry. So many things were hitting me at once that I wasn't sure if I had a right to speak until I'd sorted them out. Even if there had been nothing else on my mind, it wouldn't have been easy. Until today, I've never told a woman I loved her."

"And I had to nearly get killed before you said it," she observed solemnly, but her eyes were laughing at him.

"No." His lips tasted hers before he went on. "That's why I wanted to talk to you tonight." He tugged her blouse from the waistband of her skirt and slipped his hand inside to press warmly against the bare skin of her back. "I decided to tell you and let the chips fall."

Molly sighed as she freed the top button of his shirt. "What chips?" she inquired.

Gazing deeply into her eyes, he stilled her roaming hand with his. "I'm not interested in a live-in arrangement. I've never been in love before, and I want it all, starting with marriage."

She smiled softly. "That's sort of what I had in mind, too."

His eyes clouded. "Molly, you told me that 'want' wasn't enough anymore. Are you sure that love is?"

She smoothed the hair off his forehead. "Yes. We're not your parents, sweetheart. If we love each other enough, we can make it work. I don't relish the idea of your being away from home half the time, but I can live with it."

"Maybe you won't have to." She lifted a brow, and he went on. "Monarch Oil wants to buy Delaney Drilling. Dirk and I are going to meet with them when I get back to Houston. Dirk wants to settle down with Suzanne." He made a wry face. "He told me so, but I had to digest it for a few days before I could believe it. I never thought he'd let the company go."

"Love changes things," Molly murmured.

He shifted her to his side and nibbled at the lobe of her ear. "It sure does."

"What will you do if you sell the company?"

"I could retire at thirty-two, if I wanted to. Which I don't. I couldn't stand not working. I might free-lance as a consulting geologist. That way I could pick the jobs I want and take time off whenever I choose, like when you have your two-month summer vacation."

She gave him a lazy smile. "Sounds perfect."

"There's only one problem. We'd have to live in Houston, where my contacts are."

A gleam of amusement lit her eyes. "Houston isn't a foreign country. I'll bet they even have school counselors there."

"You wouldn't mind leaving your job in Dallas?"

"Not in the least. In fact, I think I'll call my superintendent tomorrow and resign. I might even be able to find a job in Houston before the school year starts."

"I thought you might wait till midterm to go back to work. We have to get you moved to Houston and look for a place to live. My apartment's too small. How do you feel about a house with a yard?"

"Wildly enthusiastic. I want a cat."

"I don't do cat litter."

"Nobody asked you."

He kissed her nose. "There's also the wedding to plan. How long will that take?"

Laughing, she traced his bottom lip with a finger before she kissed it. "A month at most." She found the second button on his shirt and loosened it, then moved down to the third.

"I'll beat Uncle Dirk to the altar." He pressed his lips against her throat.

"Will he mind?"

"Don't know. Don't care." His tongue explored the hollow at the base of her throat.

"I don't want a fancy wedding. I hope you don't."

"Love, all I want is you."

She sighed. "We'll be so happy, Chet."

His kiss was a commitment and a vow.

* * * * *

IT'S A CELEBRATION OF MOTHERHOOD!

Following the success of BIRDS, BEES and BABIES, we are proud to announce our second collection of Mother's Day stories.

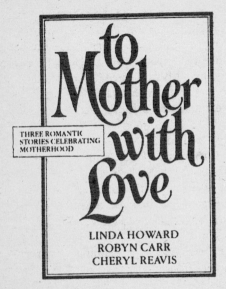

to **Mother** with **Love**

THREE ROMANTIC STORIES CELEBRATING MOTHERHOOD

LINDA HOWARD
ROBYN CARR
CHERYL REAVIS

Three stories in one volume, all by award-winning authors—stories especially selected to reflect the love all families share.

Available in May, TO MOTHER WITH LOVE is a perfect gift for yourself or a loved one to celebrate the joy of motherhood.

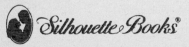

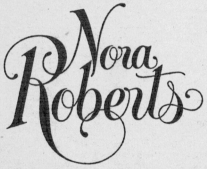